Carl Weber's:
Five Families of New York

Part 4: Queens

Carl Weber's:
Five Families of New York
Part 4: Queens

C. N. Phillips

www.urbanbooks.net

Urban Books, LLC
300 Farmingdale Road, N.Y.-Route 109
Farmingdale, NY 11735

Carl Weber's: Five Families of New York Part 4: Queens
Copyright © 2023 C. N. Phillips

ISBN 13: 978-1-64556-426-3
ISBN 10: 1-64556-426-6

First Trade Paperback Printing April 2023
Printed in the United States of America

10 9 8 7 6 5 4 3 2 1

This is a work of fiction. Any references or similarities to actual events, real people, living or dead, or to real locales are intended to give the novel a sense of reality. Any similarity in other names, characters, places, and incidents is entirely coincidental.

Distributed by Kensington Publishing Corp.
Submit Orders to:
Customer Service
400 Hahn Road
Westminster, MD 21157-4627
Phone: 1-800-733-3000
Fax: 1-800-659-2436

About the Author

C. N. Phillips considers herself to be a chameleon author because she doesn't like to box herself into just any one form of fiction. She enjoys writing them all. Born and raised in Omaha, Nebraska, she fell in love with literature when she was a little girl. She was always surrounded by books and knew that she wanted to be an author at the ripe age of 8 years old.

C. N. enjoys a great many things, but traveling to new places, cooking, and spending time with her loved ones, most of all her daughter, are among her favorite. There is something about new adventures that feeds her soul but never so much that she isn't hungry for the next one.

C. N. is most known for her daring, gritty detail and her ability to weave a story out of thin air. Currently published under Carl Weber's company Urban Books, she wants the world to know that she is just getting started. Keep up with C. N. by following her on her social media pages:

Twitter: @CNPhillips_
Instagram: AuthorCNPhillips
Facebook: CN Phillips

Chapter 1

"Ahh!"

Lorenzo "Zo" Alverez's pained shout was probably heard throughout the property. He'd just stepped into the shower, and the moment the water hit his fair skin, he felt like he was on fire. He continued to curse under his breath as he adjusted the heat. The help was always turning the water heater up when he was least expecting it. In those moments, he understood what it must be like to be a lobster dropped in a boiling pot of doom.

Knock! Knock!

"You all right in there, shithead?" his younger sister Daniella's voice sounded from outside the door.

"I'm fine. They just adjusted the water heater again."

"Pussy."

"Whatever. Get out of my suite!" he shouted over his shoulder as he stepped into the shower again and slid the glass door closed.

He heard her say something else, but he couldn't make it out over the water. It was still steaming hot but bearable. He found himself wondering what Daniella was doing in his suite, especially when her suite was on the other side of the house. Probably snooping through his things again. Ever since their father, DeMarco Alverez, was killed by the Chinese, Daniella felt the need to double-check every business transaction that Zo finalized.

The Alverez family was one of five of the most dangerous and feared families in all of New York. They ran a foolproof weapons operation in Queens that brought in a lucrative exchange. Before Marco was killed, he was the head honcho, but the hat was inevitably tipped toward Zo. Had he been ready to take on the weight of carrying on his father's legacy? No. But he was trying.

With everything going on around him, Zo was forced to hit the ground running. At one point, the five most powerful families in New York worked together in harmony. A pact was drawn up before Zo was even born. The pact called for each family to have only one trade. That way no one would step on anyone else's toes. Also, it made way for constant business to be conducted with each other, a money chain that could circle forever. The pact also stated that no family could harm another or the people they had working under them. The peace lasted for a long time, but after Barry Tolliver, another family head, was killed, everything around them altered.

At first the war had been with Barry's son, Boogie, who unleashed his rage on everyone around him. And when he finally realized the error of his ways, it was too late. He'd already lit the spark that had led them all to their current space of feuding with the Chinese, the one that got Zo's father killed.

The Chinese family was relentlessly trying to seize the power of the five boroughs for themselves. Zo still felt a fire in his chest toward them and couldn't wait to get his hands on Tao Chen. He would pay for what he did to Marco. Zo dreamt many nights of what he would do once he got his hands on him. There would be days on end of torture drawn up specifically for him. But until then, Zo was just trying to keep everything afloat around him, and that meant hiding the warehouse slips showing that their last two weapons shipments at all locations had been short.

Zo snapped out of his trance and stepped backward out of the kitchen. Whoever had killed them must have still been in the house, but how had they gotten in, and past security undetected at that? It had never happened before as long as Zo had lived. His mind quickly went to finding his mother and Daniella. He turned around to run and find them, but he was stopped by a gun pointed dead in his face.

"Going somewhere?" a voice asked right before someone crept up behind him and knocked him out cold.

Copper. That was what the blood on Zo's tongue tasted like right before he spit it out. He had come to, but he barely had time to adjust to his surroundings before he was on the defense. His arms were tired as he tried to block the punches and kicks from three big men holding him captive. He could tell by their accents that they were Jamaican, but what he couldn't figure out was why they had broken in. They were relentless in their beatings, and at first his arms were on fire, but they quickly turned numb. He couldn't feel them to send them the strength needed to keep holding them up. His mother's prized white living room carpet was stained with his blood, and Zo knew seeing it would break her heart.

"Stop!" a voice boomed.

Instantly the blows ended, and the men moved back. Stepping from the kitchen was a husky Jamaican wearing a ruby red suit. He sported freshly twisted locs on the top of his head and a shaggy beard. The designer suit he wore didn't mask the obvious fact that he was rough around the edges. In his hand was a bottle of brandy, from which he took a big swig before tossing it to the ground, shattering it. Zo blinked the blood from his eyes and focused on the man as he got closer. He was taken aback when he saw that he recognized him. It was Jahmar Brown, a man who was born and raised in Queens. He'd moved and was supposedly a big thing in Boston now. Zo's family had been doing business with him for years. Why would he want to see Zo hurt?

"What the fuck do you think you're doing, Jahmar?" Zo panted, still trying to catch his breath. "You know who I am and what I can do to you!"

"I know who your father *was*." Jahmar's tone was low and menacing. He stepped closer to Zo and shook something in his hand like dice. "And I also know who he isn't anymore. He's dead."

"So you break into his family home to . . . what? Rob us of petty things?"

"I did see a few things that will be coming with me when I take my leave. But no, that's not why I'm here."

"Then tell me what you want."

"Before Marco's untimely end, I placed an order for a hundred thousand dollars' worth of weapons. Weapons that never came."

"If that's all this is about, I can get you your weapons. And I'll think about forgiving you for everything you've done so far."

To Zo it was a sensible offer. So much had already happened, and he just wanted them to leave. He didn't want anything to happen to his mama or his sister. He couldn't lose them, too, even if that meant letting the Jamaicans go untouched.

Jahmar looked at his men, and they all began laughing together. Jahmar stopped laughing abruptly and spat in Lorenzo's face. "That's what I think of your words."

"You're going to regret that," Zo said as saliva trickled down his face. Jahmar backhanded him so hard that his head snapped to the side. He forced the pain down and took a deep breath before glaring back into Jahmar's dark eyes. "You're going to regret that too."

"Am I supposed to fear a man who is at my mercy?" Jahmar scoffed. "I was supposed to jump for joy when the only thing offered to give me are the guns I paid for?"

"Isn't that what you're doing all of this for?"

"It was, until I saw a bigger picture being painted in front of me."

"And that is?"

"Queens. I want all of Queens."

"Here we go with this shit," Zo groaned. "You motherfuckas and your thirst to control one of the five boroughs is starting to piss me off. Even with me dead, do you think my family will let some fucking Jamaican come and take my father's place?"

"How sure are you that they won't? I'm not blind or deaf," Jahmar told him. "I know all about the chaos that's been happening between the boroughs. The loyalty you all once had to each other is gone. The blacks killing the Asians, the Asians killing everybody. I've heard it all."

"What does that have to do with you?"

"Your families are falling apart. It's time for new blood to rule New York. So you will work under me. I will be the new weapons distributor. You will be the one who welcomes me into the fold and gets everyone else to fall in line."

"You want to know what I say to that?" Zo asked and sucked the blood from his teeth to spit at Jahmar's feet. "Fuck you. I would die before I piss on my father's memory like that."

Jahmar gave a tiny chuckle and kept shaking whatever he had in his hand. He stared at Zo for a few moments, taking in the defiant look on his face before looking down at his hand. Slowly he opened it and showed Zo what he was holding. Two hollow-tip bullets rested in his palm.

"These were the bullets I was going to use to end your life," Jahmar said evenly.

"You might as well get ready to use them, because I'm not doing what you want. I can't."

"I might have underestimated you, Lorenzo. Given the fact that you are Marco's son, I didn't think you'd be as nailed to the floor as him. Now *that* man could drive a tough bargain. But you I think I know how to break. You're going to give me what I want one way or the other."

Jahmar made a motion to one of the men standing close to Zo. He left the room, and Jahmar stared at Zo with an excited glint in his eye. Just as Zo was about to ask him what was tickling him, he saw something that made it feel like a hand was making a fist around his heart. Jahmar's henchman had returned to the room, but he wasn't alone. He had Zo's mother and sister in tow. His gun was pointed at the back of their heads as he forcefully pushed them onto the living room couch. Their eyes, mouths, and hands were bound, and they both had a few bloody gashes on their bodies.

"Mama! Daniella!" Zo shouted and tried to get to them, but Jahmar's fist slamming into his face stopped him.

He was knocked back, but that didn't stop him from trying again. He lunged for Jahmar when he found his footing, but the sound of guns cocking stopped him. He was helpless as he stared at his family sitting on the couch. They were going to die if he didn't do anything. Slowly, Jahmar put the two bullets he was holding into his magazine and placed it in his gun.

"I only have two bullets, so I'm thinking one close-up head shot will do it for the both of them. What do you think?" Jahmar said, standing in front of Christina and pointing the gun at her head.

"Don't!"

"Agree to my terms or your mother dies."

"I . . ." Zo's eyes fluttered to his mama, who sat up straight on the couch.

She showed no sign of fear although she heard Jahmar's threat. She had always been strong. She and Zo's papa had been the perfect match. She might have been being brave, but Zo had never been so afraid in his entire life. He would have rather died than to see her perish in front of him. He would give anything to save her life. Just as Zo opened his mouth to give Jahmar what he wanted, the sound of someone clearing her throat filled the room.

"That's enough, gentlemen."

The voice was soft but drenched with authority. Zo's eyes went to one of the living room entryways and fell on Diana, the head of the Dominican syndicate. Her frame seemed small standing in front of the army of men she'd brought with her, but her power spoke loudly. They wouldn't even breathe if she told them not to. Their guns were pointed at the four men holding Zo and his family captive, and the Jamaicans didn't dare make a move—except Jahmar.

"You wouldn't even get one shot off before this bitch's brain is splattered all over the wall behind her," he said, jabbing his gun toward Christina. "Put your weapons down!"

"All battles have casualties," Diana said with a bored expression. "Even if you kill her, you still die. You fucking idiot. Who taught you to negotiate?"

"Bitch, I—"

"I'm going to be short with you because I'm bored and I have business to discuss with Lorenzo," Diana said and eyed the Glock in his hands. "You see that little indicator there on the side of your gun? It's telling me that you don't even have a bullet in the chamber. Do you think you'll have time to cock your gun before . . . Actually, why am I still talking? Kill these sons of bitches."

The order was out of her mouth for only a millisecond before gunfire rang out. Jahmar was the first to get hit, and Zo couldn't say that he was sad to see his body twitch before dropping lifelessly to the floor. The others tried to shoot back, but it was no use. The Dominicans' bullets ate them alive. Once they were all dead, Diana went to untie the women on the couch. When she removed their face binds, Christina looked incredulously up at her.

"Casualties in war? You were going to let that motherfucker shoot me!"

"He was never going to get that shot off," Diana assured her with a smirk.

"Yeah, yeah, yeah. You're late. I called you half an hour ago when I saw those motherfuckers pay off Eduardo and the rest of them."

"Eduardo?" Zo asked, wide-eyed. "Are you sure?"

"How else would they be able to get inside?" Christina shook her head with a disappointed expression on her face. "Sometimes even loyalty fades."

"Mama, why didn't you say anything?"

Zo couldn't hide his shock. Eduardo had been head of security for the estate for almost a decade. He had been responsible for keeping the Alverez family safe for so long that Zo couldn't believe he was capable of doing something so terrible. What would make him turn on his own?

"It all happened too fast. I barely had time to call Diana for help or get to Daniella in this big-ass house by the time they broke in. I'm just glad Diana showed up when she did. But Maria and Thomas . . ."

Christina's voice faded in sadness, and Daniella comforted her. Maria and Thomas had been more than just employees. They'd become her friends, too. However, Zo couldn't mourn them yet. His mind was on other things.

"Why would they betray us like this?" Zo asked, still puzzled by it all.

"I can tell you why," Daniella said, standing. "They think you're weak, Lorenzo. They don't believe you have what it takes to lead them the way *Papi* did. You have to show them. You have to find Eduardo and the rest of them and kill them."

"She is right, son," Christina agreed. "Your father was a strong man. He would not tolerate such insubordination, especially something that would put his family at risk. You will handle it?"

"I will, Mama."

"That brings me to what we need to discuss," Diana butted in. "Coincidentally, I was already going to head over here tonight, Caesar's orders. He fears that the Chinese may be planning another attack after their last failed attempt on his life. And after what happened at his event, we both agree that we're too old to be on the front lines. It's time."

"Time for what?" Zo asked.

"This is your war to fight. It's time for the next generation to take over completely."

Chapter 2

"It's all my fault. This is all my fault."

Boogie Tolliver never thought taking over his father's empire would create so much sadness in his life. He'd gone from the prince to the king of Brooklyn. He never wanted the crown, but it was on his head nevertheless. He held his face in the palms of his hands as he listened to the beeps of the machines connected to his girlfriend Roz's body. She'd been in a coma for days since she'd been shot. What was supposed to be an event celebrating New York's godfather, Caesar King, had ended in chaos and a lot of death. Boogie was hoping that the last casualty wouldn't be Roz. But with each moment that passed, she didn't seem to be making any progress. She'd lost so much blood, and even with the blood transfusion she'd received, her survival was still up in the air. He was coming to terms with the fact that no matter how much shouting at the doctors he did or how many prayers he sent up, it was out of his hands. Boogie hadn't seen or spoken to anyone since the day she was shot. He barely left her side. He'd felt regret before but never like that. If Roz died, he wanted to go right along with her.

"God, I know you can hear me. Don't take her from me, please. Bring her back. I'll do anything. Just bring her back to me. I don't have anything else."

"You have a lot of things. Including the mess you still need to clean up out there in the streets."

The voice came out of nowhere, but Boogie didn't need to look to know who it belonged to. He wiped his face and stood up with his back still turned toward the door.

"How did you find me, Caesar?"

"You were never lost. You've been here every day for the past week nonstop. Do you think you've been alone this whole time?"

"So you've been stalkin' me?"

"No, I've been protecting you. I've kept this entire hospital surrounded with men ever since Roz was admitted."

"I don't need your protection! Don't you know that all this street shit is the reason why I'm in this situation? I just want to go back to the way life used to be!"

"The blood that's running through your veins is why you're in this situation. And no, unfortunately we can't go back to the way life used to be. And admittedly, you had quite the hand in that. In fact, that's the reason you need all the protection you can get. Especially now."

There was something about the tone in Caesar's voice that made Boogie turn around. As usual, the elder man was sharp and dressed in a suit. The diamond cuff links shined under the bright overhead light. He looked to be back to himself after being badly wounded. He also had gotten his weight back up. There was a troubled expression on his face, and Boogie knew something had happened.

"What do you mean especially now?"

"It's Tao."

"He made another hit?"

"No. He's dead. His body was found hanging from a light pole in front of his own restaurant."

"Damn. Was it one of ours who did it?"

"My people know better than to act without an order. And I checked with the other boroughs, including yours. It was none of ours."

"Then who? Who would be bold enough to kill him and string him up in front of his own business?

"I did some digging. And rumor has it that it was Ming. His son."

"What?" Boogie asked, surprised.

"Why do you look so shocked, especially after everything you've been through? The allure of power has made man do worse."

Caesar was right. One thing Boogie knew by then was that sometimes family would be the one to stab you in the back. He shook the thoughts of his mother from his mind. Trying to understand what she had done would always drive him to the brink of insanity. He would never understand.

"I guess the question that I really should be asking is why."

"I can only guess. And that guess is that he did it to send a message to the rest of them. To follow him or end up just like Tao."

"I thought they were big on loyalty and shit like that."

"They're loyal to the Triad, and now I have reason to believe that Ming has their full backing. . . ." His voice trailed off, and he looked away.

Boogie knew the look on Caesar's face. It was the look of a man who didn't want to deliver bad news. A part of Boogie didn't want to ask, but another part knew he would find out what it was one way or another.

"There's somethin' else, isn't there?"

"Roz's home. It was burned to the ground last night."

Boogie heard him but not with his ears. He heard Caesar with his body. He froze and sat on the words for a couple of seconds. The somber look in Caesar's eyes made Boogie almost afraid to ask.

"Bentley and Amber?"

"They weren't there. Bentley dropped the baby off to Morgan yesterday morning and then went to handle the affairs you've been neglecting."

Boogie ignored the slight dig and took the moment to be grateful. Roz wouldn't have forgiven him if something had happened to her brother or her child. However, his relief didn't take away the fact that someone was sending him a message.

"My men?" Boogie asked, speaking about the soldiers who patrolled his entire block.

"They unfortunately didn't make it. Your street is taped up. It wouldn't be wise to go back there."

"If you said the house is burned to the ground, there's no reason to anyway. I guess there's no need to ask if the Chinese were behind this."

"Even if we didn't already know, they made sure that we would. They left this behind on your sidewalk."

Caesar pulled out his phone and showed Boogie a picture. Drawn on his sidewalk was a circle, and in the middle was a Chinese symbol. When Boogie looked closer, he realized that the symbol had been drawn in blood.

"What does this mean?"

"It's the symbol of the Triad. I think they're warning us that this is just the beginning," Caesar told him, placing his phone back in his pocket. "I know you're going through something right now, son. But that doesn't mean the world outside of this hospital stopped. We're at war. A war—"

"That I created, I know. I remind myself about that enough. I don't need you to do it for me."

"If you know, then why aren't you out there fighting it? If you started it, you can end it."

"How?"

"That's something you and the others can figure out."

"Me and the others?" Boogie tried to make sense of the words.

"Diana and I have fought enough wars and lost enough friends. The time for us to rule has come and gone. It's time for the next in line to take your seats on the throne and put New York back together again. Hopefully you'll do a better job than us. Roz will be fine. I'll make sure of that. But you need to go, Boogie. The others will be waiting for you."

Caesar left the room, and Boogie stood there dumbfounded. He felt like a child who had just been told to figure it out on his own. He looked back at Roz and smiled sadly. She looked so peaceful, like she was having the nicest dream. Boogie went over to her and kissed her gently on the forehead.

"I have to go, baby. I have to clean up my mess. But I'll be back, I promise. You hear me? I love you."

Boogie inhaled a sharp breath, walking away from her and out of the room. He felt like he had taken so many losses that he needed a win. Caesar was right. It was time to get back in the game.

Once he was out of the hospital and inside his Lamborghini, he found himself just driving. He didn't have a specific destination in mind, but he trusted himself to get to where he was going. His thoughts were an ocean, and he was swimming freely in them. Before he knew it, he was at his destination. It was like he had blinked and had been teleported, but the truth was really just a case of highway hypnosis. He parked the car on the street and took a deep breath before looking out of the passenger window. He clenched his jaw tight as he stared at the burnt-up house. Although he told Caesar he wouldn't go there, he couldn't help himself.

The only thing still standing was the frame. Everything else was a heap of wood and ashes around it. He knew that he could just move Roz and Amber into the Tolliver family home, but he personally didn't even want to be there. There were just too many bad memories. And he didn't feel that the condo he owned was big enough for Amber to run around in. He would have to buy a new house, but that still wouldn't replace all of Roz's priceless items, and he knew that. It was the only time he was relieved that she wasn't conscious, because he didn't know how to look her in the face and tell her that once again things were screwed up because of him.

Boogie got out of the vehicle to get closer. He didn't know why, because even if he found anything he wanted to take with him, he couldn't. The smoke from the fire had made everything poisonous. He stepped over the hazard tape and began to move toward the rubble. However, before he could take another step, something else caught his eye. It was the sidewalk that Caesar showed him in the picture on his phone—the symbol of the Triad. It was something that would now be forever etched in his mind. They were letting him know that they were coming for him. There were only two possible endings, and both led to death.

"I didn't think you would be stupid enough to come here, but then again I knew you would."

The voice came from behind Boogie, but he knew who it belonged to before he turned. He'd heard it before, on that day at the big house. He turned around slowly, and sure enough there was Ming Chen standing in the middle of the street. Boogie glanced up and down for any sign of an entourage, but it seemed that Ming was alone. He returned Boogie's hard stare with a smirk.

"You must have known I was just thinkin' about how I'm gon' kill you. And everybody else close to you. You tried to murder my family."

"If I had tried to, they would be dead," Ming said evenly. "I waited until your friend and child were gone before I gave the order to burn this to the ground."

"I don't believe you."

"I wanted to show you how easy it is now for me to get through any of your security defenses. Your men are no match for mine. Even with Caesar thinking he was keeping you safe at the hospital, he wasn't. If I wanted you or anyone close to you dead, you would be dead."

"Then why am I still breathin'?"

"Are you as stupid as you look? I just said if I wanted you dead, you would be."

"So are you sayin' you don't want to kill me?"

"I do, but first I will make an offer."

"An offer? I guess I can humor you since we're here."

"I think we can come to an agreement to stop all the war and killing. You and the other families can continue to do business as you have been for all these years."

"But?"

"But you will have to pay me fifty percent of all your earnings every month."

"Bullshit. You're fuckin' crazy. I won't agree to that, and neither will they."

"Then you will all die."

"Not if I kill you first," Boogie said and reached for his gun.

Before he could untuck it, Ming made a slight gesture with his hand. Boogie froze when he saw his entire body lit up in red dots. Shock written all over his face, he looked at Ming, who was casually adjusting his shoulders in his suit jacket. Boogie's eyes went to the rooftops, trees, and bushes around him, but he couldn't spot a soul. He couldn't believe he'd been caught slipping with one of his own moves.

C. N. Phillips

"Stealth is one of the greatest tricks of my people. Sit down with the others and tell them my offer. Don't look for me. I will find you," Ming said before turning and walking away.

Chapter 3

Zo went to sleep and woke up with Diana's words on his mind. In fact, they played over and over in his head the entire day. *"It's time for the next generation to take over completely."* It was her way of officially telling him that she and Caesar were completely stepping aside. But he didn't know exactly what that entailed. Did that mean that there would be no guidance at all? Zo was still working through the emotions of losing his father, Marco Alverez, but he assumed he would have Caesar there by his side, the same way Boogie did when his father died. But it was looking like Zo was wrong about that one. He hadn't been ready to take Marco's place and could truthfully say he hadn't stepped completely into the role. In part, he was at fault for the Jamaicans' attack. He knew how to fulfill all the orders his father had left behind, but he just hadn't. A part of him was still hoping Marco would walk through the door, giving him unsolicited advice about business like he always had. But Zo knew those days were over. He needed to—

"Zo? Zo!" The sound of Daniella's voice snapped him out of his own head.

Brought back to reality, Zo remembered he was in the middle of handling some loose ends. Hanging upside down from ropes attached to the ceiling of his family's extra garage were Eduardo, Eduardo's son, Mateo, and his nephew, Julio. Zo had grown up with Mateo and Julio, and he had known Eduardo since he was a young child.

Their betrayal was one he took very personally because they had been considered family for so long. Somehow, though, his mind must have wandered off in the middle of them being beaten by his men. His eyes flickered to the floor of the garage where their blood leaked on the tarp that covered it. Zo moved his pointer finger in a circle, motioning for the three of them to be let down.

"Please, stop. Nephew, we have learned our lesson. Please, no more."

"Learned your lesson? Eduardo, you tried to have me killed!"

"I never believed they would really kill you. Not you, the son of Marco Alverez. It's true that I did something deceiving, but I knew those Jamaicans would never make it out alive. I needed the extra money."

"For what?"

"My wife, Maria. She has cancer. And since we are not US citizens, we don't have the proper insurance to cover the procedure she needs to have done. Please, Lorenzo, find it in your heart to forgive me. To forgive us. Mateo and Julio were only following my orders."

He sounded sincere. So sincere that Zo actually paused to mull over his words. He felt the glare on his face soften as he stared at the bludgeoned men before him. Mateo glanced at Eduardo and then looked down at the ground. Eduardo's eyes pleaded with Zo to hear him out.

"Why wouldn't you just tell me that you needed the extra money?"

"You were already dealing with so much. I didn't want to burden you with my crap. I should have told you, and that was my mistake. I will do anything, Lorenzo. Just—"

"I've heard all I needed to hear," Daniella's voice sounded in the garage. She walked in with her eyes shooting daggers at Eduardo. "Nobody wants to hear that bullshit sob story."

"Daniella, I'm handling it!" Zo told her, and she scoffed.

"Everybody but my brother and these three numb nuts leave!" she said to the goons standing around the garage.

They left without a second thought. Daniella turned toward Zo and looked him up and down. She didn't even try to hide the disappointment on her face.

"*Papi* would be disgusted!"

"Well, he isn't here, is he?"

"If he was, this slimy bastard wouldn't have even had a chance to speak after doing what he did to us. He would already be rotting."

"Eduardo has been with the family for years. Don't you think he deserves a second chance?"

"I can't believe what I'm hearing. You're actually considering sparing them? All because of some sob story about his wife?"

"He was once considered family. He didn't think we would actually be killed, and we weren't. We're here."

"No thanks to him! If he truly cared, he would have come back. He already had the money. All he had to do was double-cross the Jamaicans and save our asses, but he didn't. He saved himself! And, big brother, you need to learn the skill of being able to tell when someone is lying to you. Isn't that right, Eduardo?"

She went and stood in front of Eduardo. Her hand rested on the Glock nestled in the holster that was tucked inside her jeans. The way she leered down at him like she knew something made Eduardo's eyes fill with concern.

"Daniella, I—"

"What? You're a traitor and a liar? Save your words. I know. Just like I know that your wife died three months ago. I helped Mama pick the flowers out to send to your family. He told the truth about her having cancer though," she said, looking over her shoulder at Zo. "So now what?"

"You tried to have my family murdered, and now you lie to me?" Zo's nose flared in anger. The flame inside of him had been reignited. "You've worked for us for years!"

"No, we worked for your father, not you," Mateo spoke up. "He was a leader, but you? You don't know what the hell you're doing. Nobody trusts you to run this family. You aren't even fulfilling orders. And now? Now we're at war with the Asians. You're going to get us all killed."

"Quiet, Mateo!" Eduardo tried to silence his son, but Mateo didn't listen.

"No, it's the truth, *Papi!* We were going to do everyone a favor and get you out of the way before we all died following you. You're not Marco, and you never will be."

Mateo's words echoed in Zo's head over and over. He didn't even feel himself grab for his gun, nor did he feel himself fire it. He, however, did feel Mateo's blood splatter on his face. Next Zo shot and killed Julio point-blank. Eduardo was still where he kneeled, but tears rolled down his face as he looked at his son's missing face. Zo wasn't going to grant him such an easy death, no. The rage inside of him needed to be fed by causing deep physical pain. He grabbed a metal pipe on the side of the garage and walked slowly to Eduardo, dragging it across the floor.

"You think I don't have what it takes to replace my father? Huh? Well, how about I show you?"

"No—"

Eduardo's final plea was cut short when Zo swung the pole with all his might and struck him in the mouth. Bloody teeth hit the ground, and Zo didn't stop there. He swung the pole and swung again, and again, filling the garage with the sound of Eduardo's crunching bones until finally the man lay lifeless and unrecognizable on the ground.

"I'm *not* Marco. I'm Lorenzo. And I will be better than him," Zo said breathlessly, dropping the bloody pipe to the floor.

"That's all he ever wanted," Daniella said from behind him. "Whoever I just watched you become? Keep him around."

Before he called a meeting with the other families, Boogie knew he needed to be clearheaded. Every choice that ever got him into trouble was made when he was angry. No, he wouldn't just pay Ming what he wanted. It was ridiculous, and Barry would probably rise from the dead if he agreed to it. But Boogie also knew the violence had to stop. But he knew it wouldn't if the Chinese didn't get what they wanted, which was why there had to be a counteroffer. When Caesar came up with the pact it was after a long stint of fighting. He provided a solution that benefited them all. And Boogie felt he would have to do the same. He couldn't lie. He was still shaken by his last run-in with Ming. He was only alive because Ming had let him live, and he knew that. Trying to beat Ming by force might be a stretch now that he had the power of China behind him, which meant Boogie had to go another route.

It was unwise of Boogie to go into Chinatown alone, but if he had told someone what he was doing, they would have tried to talk him out of it. And there would be none of that. He was looking for information. There were a few things he didn't learn while talking to Ming, like whether Tao was really dead, and if he was the one who killed him. Boogie wanted to know exactly what kind of demon he was dealing with.

He walked down the street wearing a black hoodie. The night was still young, and the sidewalk was filled with people, making it easy for him to go unnoticed. He kept his hood on and his head down. His eyes looked for any trace of the Triad.

He stopped walking abruptly across the street from a building he recognized. It had been Li's loan shark club. Now, if Tao was dead, it was Ming's. What caught his eyes was a small symbol in the corner of one of the windows. It was the same one that had been drawn on the sidewalk in the photo Caesar had shown him—the Triad's symbol. He stood frozen. He couldn't just walk in. He was sure his face was known to them all. But how else was he going to get his answers?

While Boogie tried to make his decision, a stiff-faced Chinese man stepped out of the club. When he adjusted his black peacoat, Boogie saw the gun poking out from his pants. That wasn't the only thing he saw. The man's long hair whipped in the air as he checked his surroundings, and Boogie could make out a Triad tattoo on his neck. When he started walking, Boogie made sure nobody was watching and then crossed the street. His legs seemed to have a mind of their own as he tailed the man closely.

Boogie waited until they were passing an alley to make his move. He jumped the man from behind and threw him into the alley. When the man got his footing, he snatched his gun from its holster. Boogie knocked it from his hand and sent it flying before punching him hard in the jaw. He hit him repeatedly until the Chinese man fell to the ground, still conscious. Boogie knelt down and snatched him by the collar.

"Where's Ming?" he asked, looking into his bloody face.

"Who wants to know?"

"Me," Boogie said and pulled his hoodie down.

The man looked shocked at first and then spat blood up at Boogie. "You!" Contempt drenched his tone.

"You know who I am. Good. We can skip that step. Now answer the question. Where's Ming?"

"Somewhere celebrating your defeat!"

"He hasn't beaten us yet. And to even try, he had to call in reinforcements. Or should I say Tao did."

"Tao is dead," the man confirmed for Boogie.

"Who killed him?" Boogie asked, and the man was quiet. "Oh, you don't know?"

"I don't have to tell you shit!"

Boogie took the liberty of roughing him up some more. The last punch he laid probably broke his nose, but he didn't care. He felt like he was unleashing all his built-up frustration.

"Let's try this again. The rules are simple. I ask a question and you answer."

"My brothers will skin you alive if they find out you are here," the man said weakly.

"You know, I hate when people threaten me. It never ends well for them."

"I am expected somewhere. If I do not show, they will come looking for me."

"Then let's make this quick. What are you and your friends plannin'?"

"A new New York. Where you all will answer to us." He grinned with bloody teeth.

"Not happenin'."

"You won't have a choice. Ming is too powerful."

"Where is he?" Boogie asked again, but the man just kept grinning.

"You know, I was there when they burned your house down. It was a shame that it was empty at the time," the man said sickly. "That is only the beginning. When he returns, hell will rain down on you all if he does not get what he wants. I will tell you nothing more."

He reached down and pulled something out of his pocket. He shoved it into his mouth and swallowed before Boogie had a chance to stop him. Shortly after, he began seizing and foaming at the mouth. He was jerking so hard that Boogie just let him fall to the ground. Blood poured from his nose, and his eyes rolled to the back of his head. The scene was short-lived, and soon the Chinese man lay still, wide-eyed and dead. He had killed himself with some sort of substance. Following him had been a waste of time. Not knowing what else to do, Boogie put the hoodie back over his head and slid out of the alley before anyone could see.

Chapter 4

"Yesss!"

The piercing cry was music to Nicky's ears while his tongue made its own beat on the clit of a beautiful woman. Charlie was her name, and she had one of the fattest bottoms he had ever seen. She was sitting on his face while he licked and sucked all over her delicate kitty cat. As he was doing so, he used a hand to open her cheeks so that he could finger her anus with his other hand. Turning her on was turning him on immensely. His manhood was rock hard, and he moaned, feeling the warm mouth of another woman sliding up and down his shaft. Charlie had brought her best friend Mia along for a wild ride, promising that she would not be disappointed. And she hadn't been so far.

The women were two brown-skinned goddesses from the Upper East Side who Nicky had run into at a gentlemen's club the night before. Their lovemaking had spilled over into the morning, and Nicky couldn't have enough of the duo. He knew Charlie from their high school days. The two had never been an item, just friends with benefits. But when he saw her sitting at the bar with her friend, looking prettier than she ever had been, he knew he had to get a taste of that old thing. She still tasted sweeter than candy.

Nicky plunged his finger in Charlie's ass a few more times and then removed her from his face. He let Mia gobble him up for a few more moments before making her get on her knees. He grabbed a handful of her hair and forced her face between Charlie's thighs.

"Eat her pussy while I fuck the shit out of this pussy," he instructed.

The women looked at each other and giggled, but they listened. Charlie opened her legs wide and smacked her wet kitty before spreading it open for Mia. Nicky watched Mia's long tongue start at Charlie's opening and travel up to her engorged clit.

"Mmm," he moaned.

He watched the girl-on-girl action for a few minutes, stroking himself. He felt a small nick on his bottom lip and realized he had bitten it. That was how much they were turning him on. He grabbed a condom from the bed, slid it on, and then slid inside of Mia.

He pounded in and out of her relentlessly, reveling in how good she felt. She was soaking wet, and her walls gripped him tightly. He wanted badly to take the condom off and feel her for real, but he didn't want any of the drama that could come with that. Mia started to moan and stopped eating Charlie for breakfast, so Nicky pushed her face back between Charlie's legs.

"Don't stop until she cums all in your mouth," he told her breathlessly. "I don't care how good this dick feels. You please her just like I'm pleasing you."

He smacked one of her cheeks hard and continued demolishing her love tunnel. His moan was loud, and he threw his head back. He hoped Charlie was almost to her climax, because his stomach was cramping trying to hold his back.

"Ah! I'm cumming!" Charlie squealed and gripped Mia's head tighter.

After her outcry, Mia shouted too. Nicky saw her juices flowing all around his shaft and felt her walls contracting. He hurried to pull out of her and snatch the condom off.

He massaged the tip of his manhood right as he felt his orgasm coming and ejaculated on the small of Mia's back. It felt amazing, yet it drained his entire body of energy. He collapsed on the bed beside them and wiped the sweat from his forehead.

"You two are dangerous," he said after they had all caught their breath.

"Are we too much for you to handle?" Charlie asked devilishly.

"Never that. You both can put that pussy on me anytime." Nicky stretched big and then put on a pair of Versace pajama pants.

He wanted to take a shower, but he had one rule: never turn his back on a woman he didn't know. Especially in his own bedroom. The stories he'd heard about men getting their pockets run by women they slept with was enough for him to be overly cautious. Plus, any woman who dealt with Nicky didn't have to worry about any paper. He got up from the bed and went to grab his wallet from his dresser. From it he pulled ten crisp $100 bills.

"For a night and morning of fun," he said, splitting it and holding it out to them.

"We're not prostitutes," Mia said, turning her nose up.

"I never said you were. This is just me showing that I appreciate you for making me feel good."

His charming smile softened their faces, and they didn't need more convincing to take the money. They got dressed and fixed their natural curls the best they could before leaving his bedroom. Right when they got to the front door, there was a knock on it.

"This nigga always shows up at the perfect times," Nicky said sarcastically, assuming it was his brother, Nathan.

But when he looked through the peephole, he saw that he was very wrong. He looked at the girls and then back at the window. He was in the penthouse suite, so there was no way he could have them go out the window. He could make them go back in the room, but once again, he didn't trust anyone alone in there.

"Fuck," he said, knowing he had to just open the door. He forced a smile to his face and swung it open. "What's up, Unc?"

Caesar stood in the hallway and gave Nicky's attire and the girls one glance before shaking his head and stepping inside. He sat on one of the barstools at the island in the kitchen and stared at his nephew blankly. Nicky wiped down his face with his hand. He was a very disciplined man, but he loved pussy. It was how he'd been since he was younger. He never let it get in the way of business, though.

"All right, ladies, it's time for you to g—"

"Is that Caesar King?" Mia interrupted him and went all googly eyed for Caesar. "Oh, my goodness. You are him. Nicky, Caesar King is your uncle?"

"I'm surprised he didn't tell you." Caesar feigned shock. "That's how he used to get all of the girls to come home with him."

"N . . . wha . . . I . . ." Nicky fumbled over his words. He couldn't believe Caesar had just outed him like that. "I wouldn't say all of that. Maybe once or twice."

"Charlie might have known."

"I'm pretty sure I'm one of the girls he name-dropped you to," Charlie teased Nicky with a wink.

"Yeah, yeah, weren't you guys leaving?"

"I would much rather stay here and get to know Caesar," Mia said flirtatiously.

Nicky watched her have the nerve to bat her eyelashes at Caesar like the reason they were bent up wasn't because he had just gotten done blowing her back out. She was completely fanned out, and he made a mental note to never sleep with her again.

"As much as I would love the company of you two lovely ladies, my nephew and I have business to discuss. Maybe next time."

"Okay," Mia said.

She and Charlie left the penthouse, but not before both of them shot Caesar another hungry look. Nicky couldn't believe what he had just witnessed. He turned around and pointed a finger.

"Remind me to never bring any of my bitches around you," he said, and Caesar chuckled.

"When will you learn, boy? The ladies love a seasoned man. We reek of old money among other things."

"And I don't want to know what those other things are." Nicky shuddered and went to pour himself a glass of orange juice. "But anyway, you're here. Early as hell, might I add. Is everything straight? Something happen with the Chinese?"

"There hasn't been an attack on us since Caesar's event at Druid Hall. But I can say with certainty that Tao Chen is dead."

"Like, dead dead?"

"They found him hanging in front of his own restaurant."

"I know it wasn't one of us then. We wouldn't have been able to kill him, let alone string his ass up in his own territory in this climate. So who did it, one of his own?"

"I have reason to believe that it was his own son."

"Yo, what? I thought the Chinese had all that honor shit going on."

"That's what Boogie said. But from what I knew, Tao wasn't much of a father. And now Ming is next in line to inherit everything Tao was."

"Including the Triad."

"Yup."

"Damn. We better saddle the fuck up then. They're coming for everything. Are you ready, Unc?"

"The real question is, are *you* ready?" The way Caesar asked the question made Nicky raise his brow.

"What do you mean by that?"

"I mean, it's time. Boogie, Lorenzo, and Morgan already know."

"I hear you, but I don't hear you."

"Diana and I are stepping back and letting you four step forward."

"In the middle of a war? I . . . I don't know if that's the best idea."

"It wouldn't be if we weren't leaving our empires in the hands of four very capable people. It's time, Nicky."

"I'm not ready."

"You were when you thought I was dead."

"And I fucked that shit up!"

"Do you think this entire time I haven't made any mistakes? That I was perfect and never fucked up?"

"I don't remember any fuckups."

"That's because you view me with love, and the people under you will view you the same way. You will be greater than I ever was."

"And where will you go?"

"I'll be around," was all Caesar said, and Nicky knew he wasn't going to get any more out of him. "In the meantime, I think it's time that I introduce you to my connect."

"I thought you were the connect."

"For many I am, but I still have to get my product from somebody. And if you're going to take over for me, you need to meet him in person."

"When?"

"I'll let you know. In the meantime, how about you go shower so we can get some breakfast?"

Chapter 5

Awkward. That was the only word to describe the vibe as Zo, Morgan, Boogie, and Nicky sat in the seats their predecessors once occupied, staring at each other. They had all met in what had once been the main meeting place for the five families. They'd been there for at least five minutes, and it was quiet. Nobody seemed to know how to start the meeting. Although Boogie had his seat for a while, even he seemed to be at a loss for words.

"How you holdin' up, Boog?" Nicky finally broke the silence.

Boogie's girlfriend was shot during the Asians' last attack on all of them. The last Zo heard, she was still in the hospital and not doing so well. Sleepless nights were written all over Boogie's face. He shrugged his shoulders at Nicky's question.

"I'm here just like the rest of you," he said. "And I guess we should stop sittin' around like we're waitin' for Caesar or Diana to walk in at any moment and start the meeting. All of our territories share one common problem right now: Ming Chen."

"Ming?" Morgan said, making a face. "Isn't he just his daddy's sock puppet?"

"Tao is dead," Nicky told her and then turned to Boogie.

"How do you know?" Zo asked, leaning forward in his seat.

"He was found hanging from a pole," Nicky told him.

"Who saw the proof of that?" Zo's voice got a little louder.

"It doesn't matter who saw the proof. A member of the Triad confirmed it for me," Boogie said. "I'm sorry, Zo. I know you probably wanted to be the one to off him after what he did to Marco."

"I did. But that's just another thing taken away from me, right?" Zo exhaled forcefully from his nose and fell back.

"Wait, did you just say a member of the Triad told you?" Nicky asked.

"Yeah," Boogie sighed. "I had a brief run-in with Ming a few nights ago. He burned my girl's house down."

"I saw that on the news," Morgan said sadly. "I didn't want to bring it up until you did. So it was the Triad?"

"Left their mark and everything." Boogie nodded. "I went back. I don't know why I did. I just felt like I had to. And Ming was waitin' for me."

"You must have put up a hell of a fight with that motherfucka then. How are you still alive?" Nicky asked.

"He let me live."

"For what?" Morgan asked and then held up her hands. "I mean, I'm happy you're still here. But that's not odd to you? I mean, they just tried to kill us all."

"He wanted me to relay a message to all of you. He said he's willin' to call off the war and let us go back to doin' business as usual."

"I feel a 'but' coming on," Zo noted.

"A big one." Boogie raised a brow. "One y'all would never agree to. He wants us to pay him fifty percent of our earnings every month."

"And if we don't?"

"The regular, he'll kill us all."

"Regardless, nobody is agreeing to that shit!" Nicky exclaimed and hit the table. "Ming's out of his damn mind if he thinks he's going to pimp us like that."

"My thoughts exactly. And that's why I went to China-town, to maybe find another solution, maybe find a lack in their operation, but I didn't find out anything. Except that Tao is really dead."

"I can guess that Caesar told you his beliefs on the topic?" Nicky asked.

"Yeah. He thinks Ming killed Tao."

"His own father?" Morgan asked with a wrinkled brow.

"Stranger things have happened," Boogie said knowingly. "The thirst for power makes men do crazy shit."

"If Tao is dead, then that means Ming has the power of the Triad behind him," Zo chimed in. "Which makes sense why he thinks he can make such a big demand. Either way none of this shit is good news."

"Not at all. Which is why we need to knock him off the board." Boogie leaned back in his chair when the words were out of his mouth.

"I agree, but how?" Nicky asked.

"I don't know, but the next move is ours. Any ideas, Zo?"

Upon his being called upon, all eyes went to Zo. The truth was, he was still trying to wipe the blood of his own that he'd spilled earlier that week. He'd killed before, but for some reason the deaths of Eduardo, Mateo, and Julio left a small mark on him. Not because he regretted doing what needed to be done, but because it was a reminder of all that had changed. Zo would give anything for things to go back to the way they used to be. He looked at the empty seat at the round table and knew that it belonged to the head of the Chinese family. Ming should be sitting there. But he wasn't, because of the domino effect that had changed everyone's lives. If only they could go back to before Barry Tolliver was killed, to when the pact was law and business was infiltrated flawlessly, to when his own father was alive. But Zo knew that wasn't something that could happen, so why not the second-best thing?

"You might not like what I have to say," he told them.

"Well, lucky for you, we don't have anything else on the table. What's on your mind?" Boogie asked.

"I don't think we should kill Ming."

"You're right. I don't like what you have to say. His people are responsible for Roz bein' where she is right now. I can't just let that slide."

"In all fairness, you had a big part in this war in the first place," Zo gently reminded him. "You got your retribution, amigo. Don't you think Ming deserves the same opportunity? Before we make any hasty moves, I think we should offer Ming his seat at the table."

"Didn't you just hear what Boogie said? Ming doesn't just want his seat. He wants fifty percent of ours, too. Otherwise, he's going to take it."

"I heard him, Nicky. But even with the numbers of the Triad, Ming is a practical man. It would take years and a lot of damage control to force us to do anything. He's hoping we give in out of fear. Matter of fact, I'm sure he's betting on it. Until all families are working together again harmoniously, New York will never have a good night's sleep. The best course of action in war is to avoid a war entirely if we can. We need to show him how we are all assets to each other, not enemies."

"As much as I hate to admit it, he's right," Nicky said with a sigh. "If we keep all of this fighting up, it only ends one of two ways, all of us dead or in jail, and I'm not good with either of those options."

"Me either," Morgan said.

Zo looked to Boogie, whose jaw was clenched tightly. Zo could tell that he didn't want to agree to what was being put on the table. But what other option did they have? The truth was if the Triad was half as dangerous as what was said about them, there was a chance that no one would walk away from the fight. The best thing to do was try to work harmoniously with them again.

"After all I've done, do you really think Ming would sit at a table and work beside me?"

"We won't know until we try. Our fathers helped build one of the most solid operations New York has ever known. We owe it to them to try to keep it going," Zo told him, and after a few moments, Boogie nodded his head.

"So be it. Let's figure out how to set up the meeting."

Chapter 6

It felt like forever since Boogie felt a genuine smile come to his face. But it was ear to ear when he saw his bonus daughter, Amber. She wobbled to him as soon as he stepped through the door of his right-hand man Bentley's condo. He scooped her up and pretended to eat her neck while she laughed until she was breathless. Bentley, who was also Roz's brother and Amber's uncle, had been looking after her while Boogie was at the hospital. Although Bentley was just doing what he could to look after family, Boogie couldn't appreciate him more. So much had been going on, the only thing that eased his mind was knowing that Amber was in safe and capable hands. But the time had come to hit the block and gather as much intel as they could. It had been quiet out there, too quiet.

"My big girl! I missed you," he said and embraced her. "Where's your uncle at?"

"Right here." Bentley came from the back, eating a pack of fruit snacks. He was dressed and ready to go. The only thing that was missing was the babysitter.

Boogie looked at his watch, and it read one o'clock in the afternoon. "Where's Morgan? I thought she was watchin' Amber."

"She's on her way. Got stuck in traffic," Bentley said.

"A'ight," Boogie said and tickled Amber as he took a seat in the living room. "That just gives me a little more time to spend with you."

"One thing about Amb is she loves her some Boog." Bentley sat down across from them. "I think she likes your black ass more than me."

"You don't have to think. It's a fact," Boogie joked. "But no lie, this is my little shorty right here. This shit with Roz got me thinkin' hard."

"About what?"

"Legally adoptin' her," he said. "I'm not gon' cap, it's too early to be thinkin' about marriage, but no matter what happens between me and Roz, Amber will always have a daddy."

"That's some solid shit. When sis wakes up, I'm sure she'll be happy to hear it," Bentley commended. "But enough of this sentimental shit. What's the word? I feel like I've been out of the loop since I've been on babysitting duty."

"Well, for starters, Tao is dead."

"That's good news. Who done him in? Us?"

"Nah. It might have been one of theirs."

"Damn, this chessboard is really all fucked up."

"Tell me about it. Shit's been real quiet, but I don't think it's over. All that for nothin'? There's a catch somewhere. I need to know what they're plannin'."

"So where are we headed to today then?"

"The BX."

"Nigga, are you crazy? Ain't shit too hot for us over that way?"

"I think the best way for us to find the answers about the Asians is to ask them ourselves."

"*If* we even get the chance to ask. Those motherfuckas are gon' light us up the moment they see us in the car."

"Bentley, you don't have faith in me?"

"I gotta lotta faith, my nigga. But I'm not suicidal."

"You think I would just drive us into a war zone without a plan?"

"Then let me know the plan."

"Her name is Emiko. I found her name in one of my pop's old journals. Apparently, my father did hers a solid back in the day."

"Wait, Barry kept journals?" Bentley interrupted.

"Nothin' incriminatin'. Just names of people who owed him. Whatever it was must have been major. Because when I called, she answered and said she would meet me."

"Just like that? And you trust her?"

"Most of the things I've done up until now have been a gamble. What's one more?"

"Man," Bentley groaned. "A'ight. Let me grab some extra mags."

He left the living room right when there was a knock at the door. Boogie sat Amber down on the couch and turned a cartoon on for her so he could answer the door. He looked through the peephole and saw his sister standing there holding a paper bag.

"You're late," he said when he swung the door open.

"Boy, fuck you," she said, pushing the bag in his arms. "Where's my niece?"

"Right there waitin' for you."

"Auntie's baby!" she squealed and made her way to the couch. "What are you watching?"

Amber returned the happy cry and jumped up and down on the couch as Morgan approached. Boogie looked into the bag Morgan had brought and saw nothing but snacks and juice. Roz would want to rip his head off if he knew Amber was getting so much sugar, but what were aunts for? He placed the bag on the kitchen counter and called for Bentley to come on.

"Comin', Mother!" Bentley joked.

He appeared from the hallway and saw Morgan sitting with Amber. Boogie watched as his face softened once his eyes hit her. He also noticed how Morgan gave him a shy smile when she saw him looking at him.

"What's up, Bentley?" she asked with the attitude she had given Boogie far from her tone.

"Shit, about to run the streets with your knucklehead brother."

"Y'all be safe out there."

"You know it, shorty."

Their eyes lingered on each other's for a couple more seconds before Bentley stepped to the door. Boogie made a face at Morgan, and she rolled her eyes and went back to playing with Amber. When he and Bentley were in the hallway, he placed a hand on his chest.

"Ay, what was that?" he asked.

"What was what?"

"That whole exchange between you and my sister."

"Man," Bentley said and smacked his lips. "She's in my house. I can't speak to her?"

"Nigga, that was flirtin'. You got a thing for Morgan?" Boogie found himself laughing.

"Yeah, ha-ha it up, funny nigga. Just don't get shot up by this Chinese bitch we're about to see. We'll see who's laughin' then."

"Ay, not cool."

The smell of pee was so strong in the subway Boogie and Bentley were in. People bustled quickly by them, trying to get to their destination, not paying them any mind as they stood to the side. They were nothing but blips to everyone around them, and that was why it was the place he'd told Emiko to meet him at.

"You sure she's gon' show?" Bentley asked, looking around. "What time did you tell her?"

"Two o'clock. She is only a little late."

The moment the words were out of his mouth, he saw a woman step out of the swarm of people and walk toward them. She wore a scarf around her nose and mouth, but her slanted eyes let him know that she was Chinese. When she got to them, she glanced over her shoulder before sliding her mask down.

"Emiko?" Boogie asked to make sure.

"Yes. I apologize for my tardiness, but I had to make sure that you were really alone."

"We are. Are you?"

"Yes. If it was known that I was meeting with you, I would be killed immediately."

"Then I appreciate you for takin' such a great risk to come today."

"When you called, I knew it was the honorable thing to do. Especially after what your father did for my family years ago."

"Can you tell me what he did to put your family in his debt?"

"We were set to be deported. Me, my parents, and my siblings. My father tried to hire Barry to collect information on a homeland security officer, but he could not afford his rates. The day we were to be shipped back to China came, but we were not boarded. Your father had gotten all of our paperwork. We were US citizens just like that. We were able to keep our home and belongings. My father tried to pay him what he had, but he wouldn't take it. So instead, my father offered him a favor to be cashed in at any time."

"And now we're cashin' in."

"What is it that you ask of me?"

"We want to know about Tao," Boogie asked, and she made a disgusted face. "You weren't fond of him?"

"He was a disgrace to our people. So was Li. My father and brother back them, but I am not a fan of what they do. Of what any of you do."

"Yet you're here."

"Because I also believe in the lesser of two evils. If you're going to exist, I would much rather it go back to the way it was."

"What can you tell me about Tao's death?"

"That it has been kept on hush. I only know because my brother worked closely with him. He was guarding the door at Tao's when he died."

"Who killed him?" Boogie asked, and Emiko looked him in the eyes.

"His son," she said, confirming Caesar's words. "His son killed him and will soon be the leader of the Triad. It is something that some of us fear and others rejoice in."

"Why?"

"Because when that happens, they are certain that the Chinese will be majorly in control. Some are even calling New York 'Little China' already."

"You said some fear that happenin', why?" Bentley asked.

"The practices of the Triad have been said to be evil. Chu On is the devil. He is the reason my father never wanted us to go back to China. The things he saw the Triad do to maintain power still gives him nightmares. I, for one, don't want to live in hell, and that's what will happen."

"Maybe we can stop it. Where is Ming now?"

"You're too late. He's already on his way to China with Chu On," she said sadly.

"Dammit. Thank you again for meeting with me, Emiko. You have my number. Please use it when Ming gets back," he told her, and she nodded.

She put her scarf back on her face and turned to walk away. She stopped midway and looked back at Boogie. Her eyes smiled.

"I have never forgotten what your father did for my family. I always thought men like him were bad, but now I know some just do what they know. Like you. But it's how we redeem ourselves that matters. Kindness lives in all of us. I was very sad to find out he died. But meeting you, I know he would be proud."

She stepped away from them and blended into the crowd until Boogie couldn't tell her apart from anybody else.

Chapter 7

The time to re-up had come upon them, and as promised, Caesar had Nicky in tow. Their security detail followed closely behind them as they were en route. Nicky sat in the back seat of the Phantom next to his uncle and adjusted the cuffs of his button-up. Caesar glanced over at him with laughter in his eyes.

"How many times are you going to play with those cuff links?" he asked.

Nicky immediately stopped and grinned despite himself. His nervousness was showing. He knew how important it was for him to make a good impression. Although he was ready for his new journey, he knew that he wasn't Caesar. Anybody with two eyes could see that.

"You don't have to be me," Caesar said, seeming to read his mind. "But you are my bloodline, and that alone demands respect. Find your comfort zone in being yourself. Dom will be able to tell right off the bat if you aren't."

"Tell me about him again," Nicky said.

"Dom? He's cutthroat but thorough. Reliable and always on time with the product, so remember to always be as prompt with the payment."

"Anything else I should know?"

"Yes." Caesar's expression grew serious. "He strongly dislikes men who think with their dicks. A man easily swayed by pussy is one he can't trust."

"What man doesn't like pussy?" Nicky instinctively asked.

"It isn't about not liking it. It's about being disciplined. And that's something you need to learn. He'll test you. So be ready."

"Test me how?" Nicky asked, but Caesar didn't say anything. "Come on, Unc. If you know, let me in on it. I don't want to fuck this up."

"Then don't," Caesar told him as the Phantom pulled through the gates of an estate. It was a grand home, and there was a welcoming committee outside awaiting their arrival. There was a tall man standing front and center, and around him was his security. They all looked like they belonged in the movie *Men in Black*.

"Showtime," Nicky said when they pulled around the circular drive and parked.

After their entourage got out of the SUV behind them, their driver opened their door for them. Nicky got out first and then Caesar. The man Nicky noticed came forward, and he was able to get a better look. He was Haitian, or that was Nicky's best guess. He wore his hair cut low and had a scar across his wrinkled face. When Caesar approached him, he spread his arms.

"Caesar! Right on time!" his voice boomed.

"Aren't I always, Dom?" Caesar chuckled, and the two men embraced, patting each other's backs.

"It's good to see you, old friend," Dom said when they stepped back. "I didn't believe it when they said you were dead. I said to myself, 'That Caesar always has a trick up his sleeve!'"

"I'm glad to know that even after all these years you still have faith in me," Caesar told him and then motioned toward Nicky. "This is my nephew. We spoke about him."

"Yes, yes." Dom's face fell when he turned his attention to Nicky.

His gaze was piercing, but Nicky didn't shy away. He held the gaze with his head high and stuck his hand out.

After Dom was done studying him like a specimen, he shook it, but still his expression didn't change.

"I'm sure you'll find that he's every bit as competent and trustworthy as I have been," Caesar said.

"If you say it, then it must be true. Come, let us discuss business," Dom said and waved them inside of the grand home.

Their security followed them inside, and Dom led the way. The home had a renaissance-arts vibe, with many paintings hanging from the walls. The ceilings were high, and the sun poked through every window facing them. Dom took them to a room in the middle of the house with a dome-shaped ceiling. Each wall of the room had a door that led somewhere else in the house. There was a rectangle table made from pure gold, and around it were golden chairs with red cushions. They resembled miniature thrones.

"Always one for such opulent things," Caesar noted before taking a seat.

Nicky sat next to him, and Dom sat at the end of the table, facing them.

"What's the point of making all of the money if I can't spend some of it?" Dom commented and ran his hand on the golden tabletop. "Gold. It's one of my favorite things. I love it. Growing up in Haiti, I was poor. But I swore that when I was a wealthy man I would line my house in gold, and I did. It is beautiful, and the value of it never decreases. But we are not here to discuss my table. We are here to discuss you leaving the business. Why? You are Caesar King. *The* Caesar King."

"Two words: I'm tired," Caesar answered with a smile. "I will always be Caesar King, even after I die. But while I'm still living, I want to enjoy the little bit of life I have left. I didn't build all of this not to be able to do that."

"And you trust your kingdom in the hands of a child?"

Dom asked and jerked his head at Nicky. At that moment there was a small knock on one of the sets of double doors. "Enter!"

The doors opened, and in walked two beautiful half-naked Haitian women holding trays in their hands. Their breasts were full in their bras, and their thick bottoms swallowed the thongs they wore whole. In their hands were trays containing refreshments. One of them stopped directly in front of Nicky and bent over to set the tray down. Any other day Nicky would have been eyeing her down and wondering how fat her kitty was, but he ignored the look of seduction she gave him as she poured him a glass of brandy. His eyes were glued to Dom's face.

"Child?" he asked and fought the urge to turn his nose up. "I'm a grown man."

"I'm sorry, did I offend you?" Dom asked humorously and waved the women away.

"Yes, actually you did. Caesar wouldn't have wasted his or your time by bringing me here if he didn't feel that I was fully capable of handling the load at full capacity."

"'Full capacity,' he says," Dom laughed.

"With all due respect, Dom, don't forget that we were his age when we began doing business together. And look at everything we've built," Caesar reminded him.

"Times were different back then."

"They were, but they only worked because we worked together."

"I don't know, Caesar. I haven't seen what he's capable of."

"What I'm capable of?" Nicky scoffed. "This isn't something I just started doing yesterday. I have been pushing your work for my uncle since before I graduated high school. Me coming up in the ranks had nothing to do with being Caesar's nephew. It had everything to do with my loyalty and my work ethic. Now I could sell this shit in my sleep. I know the ins and I know all of the outs. Not only that, but I have an army of men who would die for me. The only thing we need you to do is provide the same product you've been providing for years. That ain't shit but a simple money transaction. The only difference now is the receiver."

After Nicky's outburst, the room grew quiet. And although Nicky couldn't see it, Caesar had a small smile on his face beside him. Dom stared blankly back at Nicky before clearing his throat.

"I think we're done here. You know the way out."

Nicky was taken aback by the sudden dismissal. Dom stood up and began walking out of the room. Nicky could have kicked himself in the foot. He had come on too strong. He opened his mouth to say something else, but Caesar placed a hand on his arm.

"Let's go," he said.

"But—"

"The meeting is over. Let's go."

Nicky sighed and got up. He and Caesar left the property, and it took all of his power not to let his shoulders hunch. He had just blown his one shot. Now where was he going to get a connect from if Caesar was gone? They got in the back seat of the Phantom, and he sat back hard.

"I think you pissed him off," Caesar said as the car drove off.

"I fucked up. My bad. He just called me a child, and I spazzed." Nicky shook his head. "That shit was just disrespectful, and I wasn't having it. And you told me to be myself."

"I did," Caesar confirmed and pulled out his cell phone.

"Fuck. I told you this wasn't the right time for you to be bowing out. Now where am I going to find a new connect?"

"You won't have to. Dom just texted me and told me where you can pick up the next shipment."

"What? But he just kicked us out of his crib."

"The meeting was over. He'd already made his decision. You must have passed his tests." Caesar showed him Dom's text with the location and date.

"Wow."

"That's what I said in my head when you didn't even give those women a second glance."

"Man, I'm not all about pussy. I just like it. That's all. Will you come with me?"

"Take Nathan. I won't be here. I think it's time for a vacation."

"Okay," Nicky said and glanced out the window. "This is crazy."

"Which part?"

"That you're really done."

"I don't think I'll ever be completely done. But the fact still remains, New York has a new kingpin."

Chapter 8

Gusts of wind blew past Ming's face when he stepped off his family's Learjet. He hadn't been to China since he was a child, but if his memory served him right, it was exactly how he remembered it. The warm sea air hit his nose and took him briefly to a memory of swimming in the ocean when he was a boy. He blinked back to the present and looked around at the landing site. There wasn't much to take in there, and he wondered if he would have time to explore while he was there. However, he knew it was a business trip.

Ming walked side by side with his great-great-grandfather, Chu On, as they were led to an awaiting black CEO SUV. Completely surrounding them as they walked were an array of foot soldiers ready to shoot or give their lives for either Ming or Chu On.

"You ride in this," Chu On said when they reached the SUV. He pointed for Ming to get inside. "We will meet again later tonight."

"Where are you going?"

"Home. I must rest." Chu On nodded toward another SUV parked a short distance away. "You will be in very capable hands."

Chu On walked away without saying anything else. But his last words made Ming curious. He was sure he would figure out the meaning of them soon. And sure enough, soon came much quicker than he thought. The moment he got inside of the vehicle, his attention went directly to a man sitting on the other side. He wore a gray fitted suit, and on his face was a pair of dark shades. He smiled when Ming sat across from him. The two of them seemed to be about the same age.

"You must be the cousin from America I've heard so much about."

"And you must be the capable hands Chu On spoke of. You're my cousin?"

"Yeah. The name's Hong," he said and took off his shades.

Hong extended a hand, and Ming stared at it. He then looked Hong in the face and couldn't help but to notice the slight resemblance between the two of them. Ming finally gripped his hand when he felt the driver begin driving.

"Why have I never heard of you until now?"

"You want the long story or the super cut?" Hong asked.

"You can keep it short."

"Well, the shortened version is that our family was ashamed of me. My father was a very married man who made his way to the bed of a whore, and well, here I am."

"And how is that?"

"Luck had its way, and my old man never fathered a boy with his wife. Only girls, which meant he needed an heir. Me."

"And how did you get so close to Chu On? The fact that I am here with you shows that he must trust you," Ming noted.

He stared out the window briefly at the congested traffic. Although the windows were rolled up, the smell of burnt gasoline from the motorcycles on the road snuck into the vehicle. His eyes fell on the grassy planes around them, and he yearned for the beautiful mountain scenery coming up if traffic ever moved. Ming focused his attention back on Hong right before his question was answered.

"That's an even shorter story. I had to work my ass off. I trained three times harder and did three times the work as everybody else. Worked my way up in the ranks, killed a lot of people for Chu On, and now I'm one of his most reliable. So reliable that he trusted me with the most important task at hand."

"Me."

"Yup." Hong winked. "I've been charged with making sure you're really up for the task."

"What task?"

"Taking Chu On's place."

"I already told him I was," Ming said, sitting up straight. "I *showed* him that I was."

His father's lifeless body flickered in his mind. Ming had killed him to prove to Chu On that he was willing to not only be the leader of the operation in New York, but to one day fill his shoes as well. He didn't think there would be any more tests.

"Becoming the head of the Triad isn't something to take lightly, Ming. It also isn't just something that's handed down. It's something that's earned. Here." Hong reached into his pocket. From it, he pulled out a folded piece of paper and handed it to Ming. "No one here knows your face, which means you can get in and out of places a lot easier than the rest of us."

There was something about the slow smile forming on Hong's face that made Ming raise his brow. He unfolded the piece of paper and looked at it. It didn't read anything spectacular, just a list of three names.

"Is this . . ."

"Chu On's kill list. He wants you to cross those names off. So buckle up, cousin. You're in for a fun weekend in China."

***

Back in New York, Zo found himself pacing back and forth in his father's study. A day had passed since he met with the others, and truth be told, he was shocked they had agreed to his proposal. What he suggested was dangerous, but so was war. So far no one had been able to make contact with Ming. In fact, things had been quiet, but that didn't mean anything. For all they knew, Ming could be coordinating his next attack. Zo stopped pacing in front of a smiling picture of his father. He would give anything to just talk to him one last time. He needed his wisdom.

"I feel like I don't know what the hell I'm doing, *Papí*," Zo said to the picture. "Things haven't been the same since you left. Our own turned against us, and I feel myself turning cold-blooded. I'm gonna do it though. I'll keep Mama and Daniella safe. I won't fail. I promise."

Zo picked the photo up to kiss Marco goodbye before he left the room, but his fingers brushed against something on the back of the frame. When he turned it over, he saw that a key was taped to the back of the picture. It looked to be the key that went to Marco's file cabinet in the far right corner of the room. Although his father was dead, Zo felt guilty for pulling the key loose and walking to the file cabinet. The key was obviously hidden for a reason, but whatever reason that was, Zo was curious to find out. He glanced over his shoulder to make sure no one was coming before he unlocked the cabinet.

The top drawer wasn't filled with anything but old porno DVDs. Zo smirked to himself. He knew why his father felt it would be best to keep something like that locked away. His mother could be a firecracker when she wanted to be, and one thing that she never was fond of was Marco looking at other women. The second drawer contained all of their legal financial records, which Zo made a mental note to go over to make sure their bank accounts were in order. From the third and final drawer he pulled out a folder. When he opened it, he saw more bank statements. Just as he was about to close the folder and put it back, something caught his attention. The bank statement had a Miami, Florida, address listed under both Zo's and Marco's names. The account had a little over $2 million in it. To his knowledge, Zo didn't remember Marco ever taking a trip to Florida, let alone having a home there.

He went to Marco's desk and opened his father's laptop to do some more digging into their records. He wasn't able to find anything on the bank account, but after some extensive searching he was able to find a beach house listed in his father's name. Zo found himself flustered. Why did Marco have a home in Miami that nobody knew about? He returned his attention to the folder and flipped through it some more, hoping to find answers. He had no such luck. The only thing he found was a sticky note with a phone number stuck to the last page.

There was no name on it, just a number. He looked at it for some time, debating if he should call it. What if someone answered the phone and told him that Marco had another family in Florida? That would break his mother's heart. He wanted to let his father rest with the good memories they had of him. He didn't want anything that could taint them to be brought to the surface. *But then again* . . . Curiosity got the best of him. Before Zo knew it, his phone was in his hand, and his thumb was dialing the number. After he pressed the call button, he placed the phone to his ear and listened to it ring.

"Hello?" a man's gruff voice answered.

Zo opened his mouth, but nothing came out. He just froze. A part of him had been hoping that whoever the number belonged to didn't pick up.

"Marco?" the man on the other end asked.

"Why do you think I'm Marco?" Zo finally found his voice.

"Because he's the only person I know in New York with this number. So if this isn't Marco, who is it?"

"I'm Lorenzo . . . his son."

"Well, Lorenzo, nice to meet you. I'm Nolan. Where is your old man? I've been expecting his call for weeks. We have some business to take care of."

"Papa . . . he's . . . he's dead," Zo answered and was met with a long silence.

"I'm sorry to hear that," Nolan said with a sigh. "Well, if he's dead, then it's only right to assume you're in charge now, correct?"

"Correct."

"I usually don't like to do business with new people, but you have something that I need."

"I'm sorry. Exactly what kind of business did you conduct with my father?"

"That's a really silly question coming from the son of DeMarco Alverez," Nolan chuckled.

"Were you his—"

"I think the questions that you have best be answered in person. Can you meet?"

"I don't even know who the fuck you are," Zo said, noting how bold Nolan was to suggest meeting so casually.

"You're right, you don't. But I might be the only one with the answers you seek. There might be a few other things that you don't know about your old man that I can tell you about."

Zo hesitated, not knowing what to do. He didn't know Nolan from a can of paint and was wary of taking a risk with him. Marco had always told him to trust his gut instinct, and right then he was trying to listen to what it was trying to tell him. His eyes fell on the sticky note that had the number attached to it. It was almost perfectly placed, like it had been sitting there waiting for him. He looked back to the accounts, and curiosity took over. He wanted to know where the money was from and who it was for. And the house. Why did Marco have a house out of town? Zo's gut was telling him to take the risk. It was telling him to go to Florida.

"When?" he asked.

Chapter 9

Diana said she wasn't going to be hands-on with the feud with the Asians, but to Morgan's dismay, she was still intent on running the Sugar Trap, which would prove to be a drag. Being able to take over Diana's beautiful office was one of the only things she was looking forward to. But when she stepped inside it, holding a box of her belongings, there was Diana nose-deep in paperwork at her desk.

"Diana! You're . . . here."

"Of course I'm here. Where else would I be?" Diana said, not looking up from what she was doing. "But now that you're here, there are a few things I need you to do today. I've been looking over the books, and I see that a few girls were short on their dues this month, and I need you to collect. Can you do that for me?"

"Yes, but—"

"But what?" Diana said, finally looking up at her. Her eyes first went to the sharp teal pantsuit Morgan was wearing and then stopped on the box in her hands. "You look nice. And what's that? Did you bring me a gift?"

"No, it's not a gift. I thought since you stepped down, I would bring a few of my things to what I thought would be my office."

"Oh," was all that Diana said before she went back to looking over paperwork.

"So," Morgan said after an awkward silence fell over the office. "What's going on?"

"What's going on is I've decided to not step down. Well, not completely anyway."

"Why not? I thought you said you were done."

"That was before I thought about it. Before I thought about you," Diana said and looked up at her again. "Boogie, Nicky, and Lorenzo had someone to show them the ropes. Their grooming began when they were just boys. But you just were recently thrown in. You aren't ready to take over completely yet."

"So what, you feel like you have to hold my hand like I'm some child?"

"Yes, actually I do."

"Then why trust me in the first place?"

"Because I am your predecessor, and all that is mine will inevitably be yours. However, I will be damned if I take your training wheels off too soon and watch everything I've spent my life building go up into flames," Diana said briskly. "Now are you finished whining or do you want to hear my conditions?"

"I don't have a choice, do I?"

"You always have a choice."

"Well, if I'm still standing here, then you should know what choice I made," Morgan said, fighting the urge to roll her eyes.

"Good. The conditions are you will continue to work at the Sugar Trap and learn how to run it, not as my assistant but as the owner. You will go to weekly gun and combat training. And lastly, I am giving you permission to conduct business on my behalf in the streets. However, no moves on your part are to be made without running them by me first. Understood?"

"Understood," Morgan groaned and plopped the box in her hands on one of the couches in the office. She heard Diana chuckle. "What's funny?"

"You are," she said. "Ever since you found out you are my daughter, it's like I've gotten every stage of you that I missed out on. Like right now. Is this how you were as a teenager when you didn't get your way?"

"Maybe," Morgan pouted and sat down. "I feel like you don't believe in me."

"Oh, on the contrary, baby." Diana gave her a loving gaze. "I see great things in you. We've missed out on so much time together, and all we have is the future. So if this is the path you truly want to embark on, I have to go to all measures to ensure we have one together."

"I know," Morgan sighed. "I have to stop being so impatient."

"That's a trait you got from me." Diana chuckled again. "Anyway, how did the meeting go yesterday? Did you figure out a way to deal with the Chinese?"

"Well, since I have to run everything by you, I guess I should tell you the plan. We're going to set up a meeting with Ming."

"Oh, really? I know this wasn't Boogie's idea."

"It was Zo's. He said that we should offer him his rightful seat at the table with us to stop the feuding. You know, try to get things to go back to the way they were. If everyone can welcome Boogie back into the fold, then the Chinese should be forgiven, too."

"He's right, even though I think it's a long shot. But a peaceful resolve is always better than the bloody alternative. Keep me in the know of things."

"Of course," Morgan said, grabbing her box of things to take to her much smaller office.

"Morgan?"

"Yes?"

"How is he doing? Boogie, I mean. I heard not much has changed with Roz's health."

Concern dripped from Diana's voice and covered her face. Morgan thought back to the meeting and focused on Boogie's face in her memory. He looked so worn out, tired, and sad. But even that didn't cover up the thirst for revenge in his eyes.

"Not good," Morgan said, shaking her head. "I'm worried about him."

"Me too. We all know what happened the last time his heart was shattered. His dad's death and mother's betrayal still weigh heavily on his heart. Keep an eye on him for me, will you?"

"Will do." Morgan nodded. "I'm going to go check on those books like you told me to."

Chapter 10

Ming woke up and found himself staring at the ceiling. He had an ache in the back of his neck, and he felt like all of his blood was rushing to his head. After blinking his blurred vision away, his memories hit him like a freight train. He wasn't staring at the ceiling. He was staring at the floor, which was about two feet away from his head. That explained why he felt like his blood was rushing to his head. Ming's ankles were tied to a rope, and he was hanging upside down. Around him stood members of the Sleeping Dragon, one of the most dangerous organizations in China besides the Triad. Ming focused his attention on the man directly in front of him and recognized him as Bolin Zhao, leader of the Sleeping Dragon and also Ming's mark.

"You've made quite the mistake by trying to kill me and getting caught, didn't you?" Bolin said, crouching so that he and Ming were at eye level. An evil grin slipped from his lips before he reached back and punched Ming with all of his might. "And now I'm going to kill you and string your body up for all of China to see."

His chilling tone let Ming know how serious he was. He knew he only had a few moments before Bolin ended his life. Agreeing to carry out Chu On's kill list was what had landed him there. There was a moment of regret before he looked into Bolin's empty eyes, knowing very well that they might be the last things he saw. He reflected on the start of his day that morning.

Knock! Knock!

Ming finished fastening his golden cuff links before he went to answer the door of his suite. He decided it would be best to stay in a hotel in Hong Kong while he did what Chu On asked of him. It had been dangerous work, but so far Ming had managed to cross two names off the list in only three days. Po and Donghai Wu were brothers and very powerful businessmen. They'd been trying to blackmail Chu On for money and higher positions of power. Ming didn't care to ask what it was they had on Chu On. He could only imagine all of the shady things the old man had done in his lifetime. Ming just did what was asked of him and ended the two men's lives, Po with a bullet through the skull and Donhai with a knife through the chest. With them out of the way, there was only one more name on the list.

Ming opened the door to his suite and saw Hong standing in the hallway. Ming stepped out of the way to let Hong inside. He had two men with him, but they waited outside in the hallway. Ming let the door slam shut and went back to getting ready. Hong walked around the suite and nodded his head at the luxury.

"This is a nice place. Still, I'm shocked that you chose to stay here and not at the family mansion."

"I am moving around blind, only with instructions from you and Chu On. Me staying there would be dangerous. Plus, I work better when I am alone."

"Understood," Hong said. "Speaking of work, good job so far. I have to say, even I am impressed with your efficiency. Po and Donghai thought they were untouchable. And for a second there I almost thought they were too. You proved everyone wrong though. And it was clean. There is some chatter that it was Chu On's doing, but chatter is chatter. You know what they're calling you?"

"No."

"The Ghost. Because nobody saw you go in or out for either kill. They only found the bodies. Who taught you how to move like that? Like a ninja from the old days."

"My father. He trained me to move like the wind."

"Well, he did a hell of a job," Hong commended, and Ming snorted slightly. "Or maybe he didn't. Want to talk about it?"

"No. I want to get this last job done."

"Very well then. That's actually what I came here to talk about," Hong said, taking a seat on the couch. "Those first two were a walk in the park compared to Bolin Zhao. There are some who call him a demon."

"And what do they call Chu On?" Ming asked, and Hong looked him dead in the eyes.

"The devil," Hong answered with a serious expression, but then he shrugged it away. "Others call him a savior."

"Why?"

"You don't get to where Chu On is by hurting everyone. He has helped his fair share as well."

Ming turned away and grabbed his suit jacket from a chair in the dining room. He put it on, and by the time he turned back around, Hong was holding out a piece of paper to him. Ming took it, half thinking that it was more names added to Chu On's kill list. However, when he looked, all he saw were a photo and a scribbled address.

"That is Bolin, and that is where you'll find him," Hong explained.

"What is this?"

"It's a dojo. It is where the Sleeping Dragon likes to hang out."

"The Sleeping Dragon?" Ming had never heard the name before.

"Oh, that's right. You don't know. I keep forgetting that you aren't from around here," Hong said in a harsh tone, and Ming didn't take well to it. "The Sleeping Dragon is among the most ruthless gangs in Hong Kong."

"Tell me more about them."

"Well, for one, they don't use guns. The only weapons they use are shiny and sharp. To them it makes their kills more honorable. And for two, they kill for sport."

"And where is the honor in that?"

"In the hunt. Being the victor in such a form of killing makes you a warrior in their eyes. The only thing is they have been getting beside themselves lately. Their most recent kills have been a cause for much concern. Chu On has moles in law enforcement, but even still the eye of the law has been much more watchful on everyone. I'm sure you can guess why that is bad for business."

"So Bolin has to die."

"Exactly."

"And you are certain that he will be here?" Ming said and shook the piece of paper in his hand slightly.

"No. But it is a good start."

Ming blended in on the busy street as he cased the dojo. He was just a blip in an ocean of people, and that made it easy to remain unseen as he walked back and forth studying the building. He had to figure out how he was going to get inside. Going through the front door was not an option. There were four huge men standing guard outside of it. Although they were talking and laughing with each other, Ming was sure they wouldn't take lightly to a stranger walking up to them. On the third walk by, Ming took notice of a ladder that led up the side of the building and to a top-floor window. Without being seen, he slid into the alley that led to the ladder. He glanced over his shoulder and walked quickly to the ladder. He prepared to jump up and climb, but footsteps headed his way stopped him.

"What the hell do you think you're doing back here?"

Ming turned and saw a man with an angry expression staring at him. His hand was rested on the jian sword on his waist. Ming placed his hands in the air and looked behind the man to make sure he was alone.

"I apologize deeply. I just heard this was the best dojo in all of Hong Kong. I wanted to see for myself."

"Then you go through the front door to be tested. Only the best are allowed to step foot inside."

"Tested how?"

"You fight to the death! But I doubt you will have that option. Trying to sneak into the Sleeping Dragon's dojo is forbidden and is punishable by death!"

On his last word he tried to make a grab for Ming, but he was too quick for him. Ming moved with the quickness of a tiger and the agility of a snake. First, he disabled him by kicking him so hard in the ankle that it bent. Before he could fall crashing into the ground, Ming had him in a choke hold. The man tried to resist, but Ming punched his side repeatedly until he heard his rib crack. Before the man could cry out in pain, Ming placed his hand firmly on his mouth.

"Where is Bolin?" he asked as he squeezed his arm tighter around his throat. "I am going to remove my hand from your mouth, and you are going to tell me. Try anything else and I will kill you. Do you understand?"

The man nodded. Slowly Ming's hand moved from his mouth. Just as Ming thought he was about to tell him what he wanted to know, the man took a deep breath and started to shout. Ming's reaction was quick, and he snapped his neck before anyone could hear him.

"Idiot," he said.

He dragged the lifeless body behind a dumpster in the alley and went back to the ladder. He moved fast, not wanting another mishap to happen before he even *met his mark. When he got to the window, he peeked inside and saw that it led to a hallway. It was empty, but he didn't know for how long. He tried the window, and it opened easily for him to climb through. Once he was inside, he moved quietly. He could hear the small echoes of the classes taking place traveling up from the first floor. He looked around and could tell the top floor was the executive level. It was very open. There were comfortable lounge chairs, a bar, and a few TVs on the walls. On one of the tables, he saw a still-lit Cuban cigar, which meant the room had just been occupied. He had to be hasty. There was a hallway that led to what looked like an office. He thought it would be a good place to start.*

When he got to it, the door was slightly ajar. He could hear someone talking in Cantonese, and the voice sounded angry. Ming peered inside and saw a man sitting at a desk holding a phone to his ear. He was the man from the picture Hong had given him. It was Bolin. He seemed to be alone in his office. His brow was wrinkled, and he didn't look happy at all.

"You are taking too long to do what I have asked of you!" Bolin said, switching to English. "Chu On's days are numbered, and when the glorious day of his death finally comes, I will be the most feared in all of China!"

Ming casually opened the door completely to the office and shut it quietly behind him. Bolin watched with wide eyes as his office was invaded by a stranger. Ming politely waited for him to finish his conversation, all while looking him dead in the eyes.

"I have to go, but I will be in touch," Bolin said and disconnected the phone.

"You shouldn't do that," Ming told him.

"Do what?"

"Lie. You won't be talking to him again, or anybody else for that matter."

There was something about the coldness in his voice that made Bolin's eyes flicker to the door. Ming smirked when he saw the look of fear cross his face. The problem with powerful men was that they always assumed they were untouchable. They had a God complex. Bolin thought he was so safe in his own place of business that he didn't even have security at the door. It would go down as his biggest mistake.

"Who are you?" Bolin asked.

"That does not matter."

"I can assume you are only here for one thing. And whatever they offered you, I can double it. Just say the word."

"You don't have enough money to change the fact that you are going to die today. Because what I was offered for your head is priceless," Ming said and pulled out his gun.

He wanted a clean and quiet kill so that he would be able to slip out as easily as he had slipped in. He watched Bolin's every move as he screwed the silencer on his gun. Bolin's eyes flickered to the door behind Ming again, and Ming smirked.

"Make your peace with what is about to happen and what is to come. No one is going to come in and save you."

Ming aimed his weapon. To his surprise, the scared expression on Bolin's face turned into a smile. And then that smile turned into a sinister laugh.

"Nobody has to come in and save me because he never left."

Ming heard a creak behind him, and before he could turn around, a fist came barreling into the back of his head. A small sputter came from his mouth, and he *dropped to the floor instantly. His gun flew from his hand and slid across the room. He groaned as he rolled over to see who had hit him. The man standing over Ming was the size of a sumo wrestler. He peered down at Ming with a twisted smile on his face. Ming looked back to see where he had come from. He realized Bolin hadn't been glancing at the office door. He'd been looking at the closet, which was right next to it. That door was wide open, and Ming could rightfully guess that was where fatty had come from. Bolin kneeled beside him and shook his head.*

"Do you think I would be foolish enough to ever be alone, even in my own establishment, after what happened with Po and Donghai? That was no coincidence, and I did not want to take any chance. And as it seems, I was smart to think that way."

Bolin gave the fat man a hand motion, and before Ming could do anything else, he was knocked out cold.

Ming saw Bolin leering at him when he blinked himself back into the present. His vision was still blurring here and there, but he was able to make out his surroundings. They were in one of the rooms inside of the dojo. The wall to his far right was filled with all sorts of knives and swords. On a table nearby the wall he spotted his gun. Although the Sleeping Dragon normally fought with swords, maybe Bolin was planning to kill Ming with his own weapon.

"Now that you know I am not one to be trifled with, I'm going to ask you one time who sent you," Bolin said, flexing his hand. He waited a few seconds for Ming to answer, and when he remained silent, Bolin punched him again. "Before you die, you *will* tell me who sent you. I will break you."

He stepped back and gave the okay for the men around him to have their way with Ming. Before they laid any hands on him, Ming took a deep breath. He then closed his eyes and forced himself into a deep meditative state. What Bolin thought would be an easy task would prove to be one of the hardest he'd ever tried. He didn't know who Ming's father was and the physical pain that was inflicted on him every day because a part of his training coming up was how to withstand torture. Ming's pain tolerance was three times the normal man's, and while his body was being beaten like a punching bag, his consciousness didn't feel a thing.

"Stop! He's limp. I think he's dead," Bolin shouted. "You idiots killed him before I found out anything."

Ming remained still. Not even his chest moved as he breathed. Bolin was still saying curses to his men when he approached him, and he learned his error the moment he was within arm's reach. Ming's eyes shot open, startling Bolin and making him jump slightly. Ming used his body to swing toward him to reach in his pocket with one hand and snatch his jian sword from its holster. In another quick motion, Ming swung the sword and cut the rope around his ankles. He fell on his back to the floor and hurried to defend himself against the four men rushing to attack him. He held Bolin's sword out, and there were loud clanking sounds as theirs hit it powerfully. Ming hadn't fought with a sword in a while, but there was nothing like good practice.

"Aghh!" he shouted as he pushed them back and got to his feet.

Bolin stood to the side and watched amusingly as Ming was set to go against his guard.

"You are about to face the fiercest fighters of the Sleeping Dragon. Tell me who sent you and I will make sure they keep your head attached to your body."

"How about I sever theirs instead?" Ming asked and charged at the fighter nearest him.

His sword moved so fast that the man barely had time to block the attack. Ming's speed after enduring so much pain caught them all off guard, and that worked to his advantage. Ming brought the sword up like he was about to strike at his neck, and when the man went to block that, Ming plunged the sword deep into his stomach and snatched it back. The man hadn't even fallen to the ground before Ming was off and fighting the other three. Their swords clinked against his as he gave them the match of their lives. He drove them back to the weapons wall with his elite fighting skills. When they were close enough to the wall, he ran and slid between them to the table holding his gun. They lunged at him, trying to kill him before he had time to fire, but they weren't fast enough. He fired the gun three times, sending his bullets into their skulls and making them drop hard to the floor.

Ming focused his attention on Bolin and realized no more talking needed to take place. Bolin must have realized it too, because he took off for the exit. Ming fired his weapon, catching Bolin in the ankle, immobilizing him. He slowly walked to where Bolin was trying to scoot out of the room and shot him in the back.

"Ahhh!" Bolin shouted when Ming used his foot to turn him over. "I will give you anything. All of the riches you could ever imagine. Just please spare me."

"I already told you, what I want is priceless," Ming said and looked back at the other men he'd killed. "But I changed my mind. I will spare you."

"Thank you. Thank you."

"I will let you all keep your heads," Ming finished and shot Bolin point-blank in the neck.

Ming walked through Chu On's mansion and ignored the eyes of the help on him and his bloody attire. He knew he looked like cow dung, but he did not care. He passed many beautifully constructed pillars and colorful gardens on his search for Chu On, finding him sitting outside next to a small koi pond. Ming said nothing to interrupt the peace. Instead, he sat cross-legged across from him and allowed the old man to finish his meditation. After some time went by, Chu On lifted his arms and began to move them side to side in a fluid motion. It was like he was bending the air around them.

"Great-great-grandson, did your father ever tell you the story of our family?" Chu On asked, still moving his arms with his eyes closed.

"No."

"Then I will tell you. A long, long time ago, in the ancient times, it was said that our ancestor Nianzu was a general of an army of thousands. That same army was called forward to protect a proclaimed empress against those who wished to overthrow her. They were outnumbered and would easily lose in combat. With only days before the opposing army arrived, Nianzu came up with a plan to trap their adversaries. With the empress's permission, they evacuated the people of the village and cleared the palace. Then they built a sliding wall of the thickest and strongest bamboo at the entrance of the village. When the army finally arrived and ran through the village ready to slaughter everyone, they were met with emptiness. And before they could realize they had walked into a trap, Nianzu ordered his soldiers to slide the wall at the entrance shut, trapping the army."

"Then what happened?" Ming asked.

"The entire village had been . . . what do the Americans say? Oh, yes, it had been booby-trapped with gunpowder. Nianzu gave them the order to blow the village up and kill everyone inside. The empress was sad to see her village go up in flames, but she was happy that all of her people were safe. And for that, she said to him, 'I have lived hundreds of years, but never have I seen what I witnessed today. No other army would come and defend a village with a self-proclaimed empress. But you stood tall in the face of danger, absent of all fears. You are worthy of my gift. When I am dead, you must consume my ashes quickly, for I do not wish to come back. If you do, your bloodline will live on forever as warriors and leaders. This I promise you. Please, take care of my people.'

"After saying those words, the empress took Nianzu's sword and stabbed herself through the heart. But when her body hit the ground, it lit on fire and turned to ashes. The empress had been a phoenix all along. Nianzu did what he was told. He scooped her ashes into his water canteen before she could be reborn, and he drank them. He went on to become one of the most powerful dictators in all of China."

"Do you believe that story?" Ming asked.

"Pieces of it," Chu On admitted. "But it is the story of our family, and one cannot deny facts. Afterward, Nianzu, his sons, and their sons, so forth and so on, were warriors and always held much power in their fists. And now it is time for you to take yours."

"Aren't you going to ask me if I completed the tasks you asked of me?"

"I know you did. I can smell the blood on you." Chu On opened his eyes and smiled. "You have proven to me that you are ready. My body is tired. *I* am tired. You will make a good leader. A fair one. Not too tough, but not weak at all. I ruled with an iron fist. You will rule with guidance. It is time that I publicly name you my successor. Your ceremony will take place in two days. And then you will have all of the Triad at your side for as long as you breathe. Now go rest and get your strength back. You have earned it."

Chapter 11

When Zo arrived in Florida, he didn't know what he was in for. In fact, before he even left for Florida, he knew it would not be safe for him to travel alone. He could only trust one person to come with him.

"Hey! This was my favorite Louis! Are they loco? It looks like they just threw it around. This is why I hate flying commercial!"

Daniella's voice sounded loudly as she grabbed her suitcase from the baggage carousel. Zo watched amusingly as she examined her bag for any scratches, but luckily for the workers at Miami International, there were just dirt streaks. He grabbed his own suitcase and headed toward the car rentals with his sister close behind him. There were so many people in the airport it was hectic just to get to where they were going. The only reason Zo had made the decision to fly commercial was because he didn't want their mother to find out what they were doing. She had access to all of the family jet's travel. And when Zo thought about it, Marco had to have flown commercial as well. That would explain why Zo couldn't find evidence of his Florida travel.

When they reached their destination, it didn't take long for them to get the SUV and get on the road. Their first stop was, of course, the beach house. It was where they would be staying. Zo hoped that he would find at least some answers there.

"If Papa has another daughter, I'm gonna kill her," Daniella said from the passenger's seat.

"What?" Zo didn't know whether to laugh or be concerned because she looked serious.

"I guess I wouldn't kill her. But I would be pissed off!" Daniella said and crossed her arms.

"Well, there's no need to get all worked up just yet. We don't even know what we're walking into."

"But why would Papa be living a double life if there isn't another woman involved?" Daniella asked. "That's the only thing that would make sense."

"Is it?"

"If it isn't, what do you think it is?"

"I don't know. But I would rather wait and see than assume our father was stepping out on Mama. He was a lot of things, but he loved us. He loved Mama. I don't think he could ever hurt her like that."

"Fine, we will just wait and see. As long as you know one thing."

"What?"

"I get the master bedroom at the beach house!"

"Fine. I'm still trying to wrap my mind around the fact that he left me a beach house that he never talked about," Zo said, and Daniella got quiet beside him. It didn't go unnoticed. He glanced over at her and nudged her leg. "What?"

"Papa left you everything. It's like I didn't exist to him at all," she said sadly.

"Don't say it like that. He knew I would take care of you and give you whatever you need and want."

"That's not the point."

"Then what is it? Because what's mine is yours, always. Business-wise, it was probably just easier to put everything in my name."

"You don't get it."

"I do get it. You're doing what you've done since we were younger—playing the favorites card."

"You were always Papa's favorite!"

"And you were always Mama's, but you don't see me crying about it."

"He left you specifically millions of dollars and properties, and I'm not supposed to be upset? Not only that, but all of the stuff here in Florida, too."

"You're upset about stuff that I didn't even know about or even want. And as far as the other stuff, it's business! You aren't in the field at all. You collect your allowance and get to live your life, except when you're sticking your nose in places it doesn't need to be. You're just bitching about a bunch of nothing."

"Oh, I'm bitching about nothing?"

"Yes!"

"Then how about I bitch about the fact that your last two shipments were short!"

"Once again, sticking your nose where it doesn't belong. I have it under control. That's why we're here. I think Nolan was his connect."

"Think?"

"Please shut up, Daniella. I don't want to argue," Zo said and pulled in the parking lot of Magnelia Bank.

It was the bank at the top of the statement he found in Marco's office. He parked and got out. Daniella followed him, and he wanted to tell her to get back in the car. However, she had just as much right to know any information as he did. They rolled their eyes at each other and walked inside.

"Hello, my name is Thomas. How can I help you?" a banker said, walking up to them with a smile.

"Yes, I wanted to see about an account that is open with your bank," Zo said.

"Is it your account?"

"My name is on it."

"Is this lovely woman the primary?"

"No, my father is the primary."

"And is he with you by chance?"

"He's dead."

"I see. I'll be more than happy to help you. How about you two follow me to my office?"

He waved them back to an office in the back of the bank. There were no walls, only windows. He shut the door when they were all inside and ushered for them to sit down in two chairs on the opposite side of his desk.

"All right, do you by chance have the account number?" he asked when he sat down at his computer.

"I do," Zo said and wrote the number down on a sticky note before sliding it to him.

"Perfect. Now all I need is an ID and I can pull everything up."

Zo handed Thomas his ID and waited patiently as he typed in a series of things on the keyboard. When he stopped typing, Zo watched the smile drop from his face as he stared at the screen. It wasn't replaced with a frown, just an interested look.

"Why, I . . . What did you say your father did for a living?"

"We didn't," Zo and Daniella said in unison.

"Oh, well, no matter." Thomas cleared his throat and turned the screen to face them. "This is the account that you were inquiring about. It looks to be a fairly new one."

He pointed at the account with $2 million in it. Zo's eyes grazed over the transactions and saw that there weren't many. In fact, one of the main transactions was a $2 million transfer into the account.

"Where was this money transferred from?"

"It looks like Mr. DeMarco Alverez has another account with us and . . . yes, actually it looks like your name is on that one as well, Mr. Alverez. This one has—"

"Ten million," Zo noted. "Thank you, Thomas. Can you write down that account number for me?"

"Of course," Thomas said and scribbled it on a sticky note. "Your father was a very successful man. You should be proud."

"Very," Zo said and took the account number from him. "Thank you."

He and Daniella got up and left the bank. When they were outside and in the car, Daniella turned to him.

"When has Papa ever kept that kind of money in the bank?"

"Never. Did you see the transactions on the original account?"

"Yes. They looked like . . . restaurant supplies? And I saw some real estate charges."

"Exactly."

"What does that mean, Lorenzo? What was Papa doing? It can't be what I'm thinking."

"It looks like it, doesn't it? Papa was building a new empire."

When they finally arrived at the home in Biscayne Point, Zo eyed the property. It was a very nice home, but simple, much like his father had been. He never wanted the big house like they had in New York. He always joked and said he would be okay with a one-story home that wasn't far from the beach. Zo guessed that he got what he wanted. They parked on the winding driveway and got out. Zo grabbed their luggage and led the way to the front door of the house.

"Do you have a key?"

"No, but look." Zo pointed at the keypad on the front door in place of a keyhole. "I'm pretty sure I know what the code is."

He stepped forward and pressed the numbers for the date when Marco met their mother, and on the last digit, he heard the lock click. Zo looked back at Daniella and gave her a smug look. In return, she just rolled her eyes and pushed past him.

"Wow," she said when she opened the door. She looked around at the bright home, and her eyes brushed past the marble floors and the open floor plan. Gold decor and frames lined the walls to match the chandeliers in the living room and dining room. "It's so nice. I know Papa couldn't have decorated. Is that a mink?"

"You would know better than me," Zo said, setting their suitcases down. "He probably hired somebody."

"He had to have. The Papa I knew didn't know a single thing about aesthetics. But this place? This place is a whole vibe. I'm going to go look around outside."

"Be careful," Zo warned her.

"I will," she said.

When she was gone, Zo looked around for himself. It was nice in there, and it smelled good, too. His eyes went to a plug-in on the wall, and he walked over to it. Kneeling down, he could tell that it was a brand-new refill. Marco had been dead for weeks. There was no way it should be full. Zo remained still to see if he could hear anyone inside of the house, but he didn't. Still, to be on the safe side, he pulled his gun from his suitcase to check the rest of the house. He walked around cautiously, looking through anything that seemed interesting. There were three guest bedrooms, and none of them had anything interesting inside, just furniture. By the time he got to the master bedroom, he was convinced that they had the house to themselves. However, that didn't change the fact that someone had been there, which meant someone had access to the home anytime. Maybe it wasn't smart to stay there.

He stepped inside the room and inhaled his father's scent. He stepped around the room, looking at the photos hanging on the wall. Some of them were duplicates from their home in New York, while others Zo had never seen before, like the photos of Marco in his prime, looking like the man. There were some of both Marco and Christina holding guns and looking like mobsters. Zo laughed at those and took a few pictures with his phone. He had never seen his mother like that before, but her wide smile let him know that she was happy. He moved over to a photo on Marco's dresser and crinkled his brow. It was one he definitely had never seen before, and it looked like it had been taken recently. It was of Marco and a beautiful woman. The two were on a yacht sitting awfully close to each other. Not only that, but Marco had his arm wrapped around her shoulders, and the two of them were smiling like there was no tomorrow. Zo felt his stomach do a turn. He knew the photo could mean anything, but—

"Who is she?"

Zo hadn't even heard Daniella come back in the house, let alone inside of the bedroom. He shrugged his shoulders and faced the photo down, not wanting to look at it anymore. He looked at his sister's face and could see the hurt welling up there.

"I don't know who she is. But we will find out," he assured her right as his phone rang in his pocket. He answered it after seeing who it was and put it to his ear. "I'm here."

"Glad to hear. I hope your travel wasn't too much of a nuisance," Nolan said on the other end.

"It was what you could expect as a person who doesn't know what the hell is going on around him."

"It will all make sense soon. I promise. I'm sure you want to meet me somewhere public, and I know just the place."

"Where and when?"

"The Clam. It's a restaurant on the beach. Seven o'clock."

"I'll be there. How will I know who you are?"

"Just tell them you're there for Nolan. You'll be led to me. See you then."

"That was him?" Daniella asked when Zo disconnected the phone.

"Yes."

"How do you know you can trust this person?"

"I don't know. But this is the only way we are going to get the answers we want."

"I just have a bad feeling about all of this, Lorenzo. And after seeing that picture, I . . ." Daniella put her hand to her chest. "Who was our papa? I've only been here for a little while, and I'm starting to feel like I didn't know him at all."

Chapter 12

As Boogie walked through the hospital, he got a lot of flirtatious looks shot his way from the nurses, but he couldn't say what any of those women looked like. He was there for one reason and one reason only. The dozen fresh roses in his hand proved that. His heart was aching for Roz. He just wanted to see her smiling face again and soon. He needed her.

He turned the corner to the hallway that led to her room and noticed that there wasn't anyone standing watch by her door. It made the most alarming sensation come over him, and he almost bolted to the door, until he saw her regular nurse walk out of the room. She was a middle-aged black woman named Sandra. She had some of the smoothest skin Boogie had ever seen, and she was as sweet as candy. When she saw Boogie, she smiled big at the roses.

"You are the sweetest boyfriend," she told him. "Those roses will look nice by the window next to the ones your friend brought her."

"My friend?"

"Yes." Sandra pointed back at the room. "He's in there now. Oh, and you're in for a treat!"

She winked and walked away to do her rounds, not knowing she had brought the alarm back inside of him. Boogie hurried to the room. He needed to know who was in there with Roz. And why wasn't there anyone standing guard outside of her door? His hand flew to his gun when he saw a man sitting next to Roz's bed looking at her. Not only that, but Roz was looking back. She was awake. Every feeling of unease he had went out the window. She was awake and sitting up. There was even a half-eaten tray of food next to her bed.

"Roz," he breathed, and her eyes fell on him. "I thought . . . I thought . . ."

He couldn't even finish his sentence. Tears came to her eyes, and she shook her head at him. He went to the side of her bed that wasn't occupied and took her hand.

"I'm here," she said when he kissed her hand. "I'm alive."

"How? When?"

"I woke up last night."

"Why didn't they call me?"

"I thought they did, but then . . ." Roz's voice trailed off, and she looked at the man sitting next to her bed.

"Who is this?" Boogie asked, looking over at the man.

He was a brown-skinned dude who rocked two braids in his hair and had a circle beard on his face. There was something about his eyes that was familiar to Boogie, like he knew them well, but he was sure he'd never met that man in his life.

"The hospital got hold of some of my old medical records. When I woke up, they called my next of kin."

"Then why isn't Bentley here?"

"The records they found were from when I had Amber. At that time Bentley wasn't listed. Her father was."

"So this is—"

"Adam, Amber's father." The man in the chair stood up and held his hand out to Boogie.

Boogie raised his eyebrows when he realized what they were saying. Adam had a smug look on his face when he saw how taken aback Boogie was. He probably thought it had something to do with Boogie's ego, but that wasn't it at all. He looked at Adam's hand like it had bugs crawling all over it, and then he looked back at Roz.

"I thought you said Amber's father died in a car crash before she was born."

"Wow," Adam scoffed in disbelief and let his hand fall. He had a gruff voice. "Really, Roz?"

"Boogie, I can explain. I just—"

"Told me her father was dead," Boogie finished for her because there was no other way to explain the lie.

"Well, I can assure you that I'm very much alive," Adam spoke, even though Boogie had targeted his words to Roz.

"So where the hell have you been these last few years? You just walked out of your kid's life like she ain't mean shit to you?"

"Boogie . . ." Roz said and gripped his hand, but it was too late. The anger had already set in.

"I didn't walk out by choice." Adam glared at Boogie. "I was sentenced to five years in prison. But I was lucky to get out in two and a half. When I was inside, I called when I could and wrote every day, but nothin' was ever answered. So when I got out, I looked everywhere for her and my baby girl. It was a blessing when I got the call from the hospital tellin' me to come see you. I felt like God was giving me another chance with my family."

His words stabbed at Boogie's chest. Not only that, but he didn't miss the fond look Adam shot Roz, and he wasn't going for any of that. He opened his mouth to talk, but Roz beat him to the punch.

"It was a mistake, that's all, Adam," she told him while staring him in the eye. "You and I never were a family. You know what you did to me."

"How can you say that, Roz? We were together every day up until I—"

"Up until you what?" Roz asked. "Up until you robbed that bank and went to prison."

"I did that for us!"

"For us? You did that for you!" Roz exclaimed, growing tired of the back-and-forth. She seemed to find more and more of her voice, the one she didn't have when she first saw him next to her hospital bed, and the one she should have had when they were together. "You never even wanted my daughter! And you and I both know you never gave a damn about me. You are an evil, evil man, Adam. And I don't want you anywhere near us, especially her. I moved on with my life, and you won't be a part of it."

"Yeah," Boogie spoke up. "She moved on. So you should too. I'm here now. You can go."

His tone was dismissive, and it didn't go over Adam's head. He looked at Roz as she held Boogie's hand, and there was a longing on his face. He nodded his head in understanding and made to leave.

"But before I go, Roz, I can only guess that he's the reason you ended up shot up in a hospital bed. Is that the life you want for my daughter?" Adam asked before looking Boogie up and down. "You might be a little flossed up, but you ain't no better than me."

With that he left, finally giving Boogie some alone time with his woman. He cupped her cheek and placed his forehead on hers. She didn't know how happy he was to see her eyes.

"Boogie, I—"

"It's cool, Roz. Don't stress about that shit," he told her.

"But I lied to you," she said.

"You did, but he was right about one thing. You're in this bed because you fell in love with me. I wouldn't even feel right bein' mad at you for lyin' to me about Mr. Five Stacks."

"Boogie!" Roz exclaimed and found herself laughing. She clutched her stomach. "Don't make me laugh. It still hurts."

"My bad. I'm just glad you got out of the habit of fuckin' with broke niggas."

"Yeah, and I'm gon' need a major gift after this," she said with a small smile.

"I already got that on lock. You're gettin' a new crib and a new whip. And anything else you want in between. Because you're priceless, baby. I don't know what I would have done if you didn't wake up," Boogie told her, kissing her lips gently.

He couldn't even bring himself to tell her about what happened to the house. Instead, he dressed it up nicely, and her face lit up like a Christmas tree.

"I have something else to tell you, too," she said. "There were men standing at the door when I woke up. I had the staff make them leave."

"Why would you do somethin' like that?" Boogie asked, wide-eyed.

"Seeing them reminded me of when I got shot. It just kept playing over and over in my head. I just wanted some peace. I know it wasn't smart, but they were just a reminder. I just . . . I just . . ."

"Hey, hey, hey. It's okay, Roz. I'm not mad at you, a'ight? It's good. I'm movin' you out of here to finish recoverin' as soon as I can anyways."

She nodded and scooted over in the bed so that he could climb in and hold her close. As they lay together watching TV, he made a mental note. He was sure that dude wasn't anything to worry about, but keeping an eye on Adam wouldn't hurt.

Chapter 13

The live band set the tone for the Clam as they filled the air with comforting jazz music. There were a mixture of aromas filling the air, and the dim lighting set the tone for a nice fine-dining experience. The women servers wore sparkling gold dresses, and the men wore black fitted suits. Zo had to admit, theirs almost looked as good as the Tom Ford two-button suit blessing his body.

He and Daniella sauntered side by side and enjoyed the attention the other guests were giving them. Probably more her. The one-armed red dress she wore hugged her tightly, stopping just above the knee. The stilettos in her open-toe mules stabbed the ground with each step she took. She embodied a bad bitch. No, she was a boss. A pretty, young waitress led them down a long hallway at the back of the establishment. The crystal light fixtures hanging from the ceiling lit more than their patch, but they gave them a clear look at the fine-arts paintings hanging from the walls.

"Here we are. Our grand room. Nolan is waiting for you," the waitress said and pulled back a black velvet curtain that seemed to take the place of a door.

They stepped into a party room with a long rectangular table inside of it. The table was filled with all kinds of delectable seafood ready to be eaten. On one side of the table was a white man, wearing a custom suit, diving in. Standing not too far behind him on either side were two bigger white men staring expressionlessly at both Zo and Daniella.

"Nolan?" Zo asked the man as he cracked open a crab leg.

"The one and the only. I'm glad you were able to make it, Lorenzo," he said, looking up at them with a bright smile. "Thank you, Dominique. You'll be receiving a big tip from me tonight."

The girl giggled and left them, but not before closing the curtain again. Nolan motioned for Zo and Daniella to take a seat. When they did, a server came from nowhere with plates and napkins and poured them each a glass of wine.

"Thank you," Daniella said politely.

"I didn't know what you guys like to eat, so I ordered everything," Nolan said with a charming smile. "Dig in."

Zo and Daniella looked at the food and then at each other in unison. Neither touched a thing. Zo scanned his face and tried to think if he'd ever seen him before. He was younger than Marco but at least ten years older than Zo. He had a face full of freckles and had blond hair and brown eyes. He was clean-cut and had good taste in what he wore. Zo couldn't say he had ever seen him a day in his life.

"Why did you want to meet here?" Zo asked, cutting right to the chase.

"What, besides the great food that you aren't eating and the hospitality?" Nolan asked with a grin. "I guess I just wanted to show you one of the places your father owned."

Zo felt Daniella sit up in her seat beside him. Zo found himself glancing around the room and couldn't find a hint of Marco anywhere. Not to mention he didn't even eat seafood.

"Papa owned this place?"

"He did, and now I guess it's yours."

"You mean it's Lorenzo's," Daniella corrected him, not hiding the sourness in her tone.

"I'm assuming you're his daughter, Daniella, right?" Nolan told her.

"*Sí*. I never would have thought he would own a place like this."

"Exactly. You can't come to a new city moving the same way you did in your old one, can you?"

"What exactly was my father's business with you?" Zo asked.

"Ahh, don't you want to eat before we get into all the formalities? Talking business on an empty stomach sucks, man," Nolan said, but when he saw that Zo wasn't budging, he dropped his napkin on the table. "All right, let's talk business. Your father's business with me? Easy question. I was his distro. Next question."

"Wait, wait, wait." Zo shook his head, unable to just zoom past what he had just said. "*You* are the one who imports all of our weapons?"

"Why do you look so shocked? Your father and I worked very closely for years. Hell, this restaurant will be hitting its five-year mark soon. When I didn't hear from him, I thought he had backed out of our deal. I didn't know it was because he had died. Marco was a good businessman. I am saddened that he won't be able to enjoy the fruits of our next business venture."

"And what business venture is that?" Zo asked.

"Since he died before he could tell you about me, I'm sure he didn't tell you about the plans for the future of his new empire," Nolan said and leaned forward in his seat. "Marco was going to leave New York and everything that came with it behind, besides you guys of course."

"What? Papa would never do that," Daniella said, making a face. "I could understand him expanding outside of New York, but he was too loyal to Caesar. He would never turn his back on the Five Families. It's the reason why he's dead now."

"I can only assume that he wasn't going to leave in bad business. But it is true, he was going to leave and start new here, where he would be king. The only king."

"Why would he want to do that? Papa wasn't a selfish man."

"He wanted to do it for you," Nolan said, staring into Zo's face. "He wanted to give you a fresh kingdom to rule however you saw fit. But that was just one of the reasons. The other reason is—"

"I didn't give him a choice."

The even voice belonged to a beautiful woman who had just stepped through the velvet curtain. She wasn't just any beautiful woman, however. She was the same woman from the photo. The black dress she wore stopped just short of her knees, and her heels stabbed the floor as she walked. Her brunette hair sat on her shoulders in big curls, and the lipstick on her full lips was red like blood. She didn't wait to be asked to be seated when she sat at the head of the table. She stared at Daniella and then at Zo with a look of curiosity in her eyes. Placing her elbows on the table, she clasped her fingers together and rested her chin on them.

"You're the woman who was in the photo with Papa!" Daniella exclaimed, jumping to her feet. "Who are you, eh? The woman trying to break up a marriage? Start a new life with a man you stole from his family?"

"First of all, ew," the woman said, turning her nose up. "It's crazy that you look at me and don't see the resemblance between you and me. My name is Louisa, and DeMarco was my younger brother. So I guess that makes me your aunt. And I was deeply saddened to find out about the passing of my brother. I never got to say my goodbyes."

Daniella was shocked into silence. The befuddled look was frozen on her face when she sat back down. Zo, too, was at a loss for words. He knew his father wasn't an only child, but both of his uncles had died years ago. And the aunt he knew about lived all the way in Nebraska. However, the more he looked, the resemblance between Louisa and Marco was uncanny. Same eyes, same nose, same lips.

"If what you say is true and you are our aunt, why are we just now finding out about you?" he asked.

"For one, DeMarco's mother hated me," Louisa started. "Even though I was two years older than him and from a previous relationship, she couldn't stand to look at me. She sent me away when I was sixteen."

"That doesn't sound like *Abuela*," Daniella said, shaking her head.

"I'm sure that when you grandkids came around her heart had softened a little, but back then she was an evil woman. She kept me away from my brother for years. And when I finally connected with him again, he had met Christina, your mother. She didn't like me either."

"Why?"

"For more reasons than I can count. But one of them is because she thought I wanted to take your father away from New York. Which she was right about. But with me, my brother would have lived up to his full potential instead of falling victim to our father's redundant way of life."

"Our papa was rich."

"Ahh, your first lesson. Listen to me and remember these words, nephew. There is a difference between rich and wealthy. Your father had to watch every dime he spent, because if he went over just a few cents, the Feds and the IRS would be on his ass like grass. That isn't freedom. And that was what he wanted more than anything. That's what he wanted to give you. However, his loyalty to his shackles got in the way of that."

"Maybe he chose those shackles."

"Trust me, he didn't."

"And how do you know that?" Daniella asked.

"Just a second." Louisa put up a finger and looked at Nolan. "Go get me a martini with two olives."

"Yes, ma'am," Nolan said quickly and hopped to his feet.

He moved like a person who didn't want to disappoint someone with their performance. Daniella's mouth opened slightly, and she whipped her head back to Louisa.

"What was . . ."

"That?" Louisa asked and then giggled. "Oh! You thought Nolan was the boss. No, silly girl. Nolan works for me. He is what you would call the middleman between sales."

"So that makes you . . ."

"The queen of Miami. And other parts of Florida. Marco placed his orders through Nolan, who, in turn, got all of the weapons from me. That's it. Weapons. That's all my brother brought to New York. He was worth more than just guns and explosives. He could have moved those among other things through New York, the top cocaine straight from Columbia, but no. He didn't want to step on Caesar's toes. So . . . I had to give him a little push along with my offer."

"What push?" Daniella asked.

"I started shorting all of his orders. For a while he made do, even tried to find a new weapons connect, but he learned that not many people will be willing to cross me."

"What did you offer him?" Zo asked.

"The same thing I'm going to offer you, nephew. A seat at my side. But you have to leave behind New York and everything that comes with it."

"And what is on the opposing side of that offer?"

"Join me or lose me," Louisa said calmly. "And as I just said, good luck finding another weapons distro. You'll come to learn that my reach goes a long way."

"So join you and lose New York, or say no to you and still lose New York."

"Yup." Louisa giggled again.

"This is a sick game you're playing. Why are you doing this?" Daniella asked.

"Because I want the one thing I never had but always existed. My family. Your rightful place is beside me. Not running around on that *Monopoly* board there. I'll give you two weeks to make your decision, Lorenzo. Until then, eat, and afterward I'll show you a few other things your father left for you."

Chapter 14

"Mr. King, are you ready?"

Caesar nodded at Marc, the head of his PR team, to answer his question. He adjusted the collar of his shirt and prepared to step outside to take the podium in front of many news anchors. He had called a press conference to address the incident that had happened at Druid Hall and felt that Druid Hall was the best place to have the conference.

"All right, remember, shy away from any questions that inevitably will be asked to taint your image. The world isn't used to seeing a strong black man like you with so much power in his hands. Remind them of that power." Marc patted Caesar on the shoulder, and the men walked to the door together.

Caesar had hired Marc because he didn't care about anything else but making Caesar marketable and shining light on the goodness in his heart. He was very good at his job and was one of the reasons Caesar was able to stay off the radar the way that he had. In turn, Caesar kept Marc rich and protected. It was Marc's idea to call the press conference. Although the majority of the mess had been cleaned up and cameras wiped, what had been seen outside the building was something nobody could fix. Marc felt the best way to tackle the issue was to show some kind of remorse for the lives that were lost that day.

Caesar took a breath and nodded to the woman standing by the door. She gave him a kind smile and opened it wide for him. The moment Caesar was spotted, blinding lights began to flash immediately. Their steps were completely covered with people trying to get their story. A few of them had been paid off by Caesar's team to make sure nothing was edited out. Marc guided Caesar to the podium and adjusted the mic for him.

"Thank you all for taking the time to come out and meet with me during this trying time," he started, and his voice boomed through the speakers. "What was supposed to be one of the best days of my life quickly turned into one of the worst. The people who lost their lives shouldn't have. They're saying it was an orchestrated crime of hate to all people alike. A large crowd of people like those who were gathered that day was an easy target, and I am saddened that I'll always remember that day for the massacre it was."

Beside him, Marc tried to hide his impressed expression. He gave Caesar a nod of approval and leaned forward to speak into the mic. "Does anyone have any questions for Mr. King?"

"Mr. King, is it true that the shooters were actually there to kill you specifically?" a female reporter asked.

"I don't know a single person who wants to see me dead, not even my kids for their inheritance," Caesar said, and the crowd chuckled.

"There were reports that there were gunshots heard inside Druid Hall at the time of the shooting. Do you care to elaborate?" another reporter asked.

"I was taken inside Druid Hall during the shooting, and I can assure you that there were no active shooters inside. The doors were locked to prevent anyone from getting in."

"Mr. King, your father was a known drug lord back in his time. Do you think maybe his past is catching up with you? Do you have any affiliation with illegal activities?" a blond woman close to the podium asked.

"You don't judge white kids on what their parents did, so don't do that with Mr. King. He has worked his behind off to get where he is today, so you won't go discrediting that with your ridiculous accusations, Karen," Marc said into the mic.

"Have you done anything for the families of the fallen?"

"Yes, I have." Caesar nodded. "But I am not going to disclose that unless the families feel comfortable. But the truth is, no amount of money can heal a broken heart, and I know that. I'm just happy I was able to help in some way."

He went on to answer a few more questions before he allowed Marc to pull him away from the stage. When he was inside, his PR team clapped their hands and had smiles all over their faces. Although Caesar knew he had just lied his pants off, he had made it sound good, and that was all that mattered.

"Great job at apologizing without blaming yourself," Marc commended.

"No. Thank you for handling Karen out there," Caesar said, shaking his head.

"No problem. I'm just doing my job. I'm always prepared to handle one or two of her in a crowd like that. With all these white men committing white-collar crimes and doing all kinds of shit, they're always so vengeful about how a brotha gets his money."

"And it will always be like that with wealthy black men." Caesar shook his head. "They hate seeing us at the top because they don't think we belong there. My friend Barry and I tried for years to put an end to that cycle, creating jobs and hiring a predominantly black workforce. Paid them pretty well, too. If a person wants to make money in the streets, so be it. But we always wanted to give them an option."

"That's nice, man. Speaking of Barry, I never got to tell you sorry for your loss. When I heard, you were the first person to come to mind."

"I appreciate that, more than you know. There were a few things that I wished he and I had ironed out while he was here, but you live and you learn."

"His son was here the night you were being honored, wasn't he?"

"And he's here now."

Both Caesar and Marc turned around to see Boogie walking up to them, dressed casually. Marc held out a hand, and Boogie shook it firmly. Caesar caught the eager look on Boogie's face and figured something was on his mind.

"Marc, I'm going to be in contact with you later. Make sure Erin airs her cut of the conference before anyone else does. That way if anyone edits anything out, it will be obvious."

"Got it, boss. Once again, good job out there." Marc left the two of them alone to talk.

"You have news anchors in your pockets, too?" Boogie asked, amused.

"You'll learn all the rules of the trade one day. Now what's going on? Is Roz okay?"

"Yeah, she's good actually. She's awake."

"That's so good to hear."

"It is. Your people left her wide open though."

"What is that supposed to mean?"

"I went to visit her when she woke up, and there was nobody guardin' the door."

"What!"

"She said she told them to leave, but—"

"They shouldn't have left. I'll handle it," Caesar said, but it looked like Boogie had more to add. "Is there something else?"

"Nah," Boogie said and glanced away.

That was his tell. He was lying. But Caesar didn't know about what.

"You sure?" he pressed gently.

"Actually, there is somethin' else. I need a favor."

"Anything."

"I don't want Roz holed up in that hospital. I want to know she's safe and untouchable at all times. And I still can't bring myself to stay in my parents' house for more than a few hours. Memories, you know? So until I find a new spot—"

"You, Roz, and the baby are more than welcome to stay with me for as long as you like," Caesar finished for him. "There is more than enough space. And I will bring the most capable doctors on board to make sure she heals properly."

"Thanks."

"Don't mention it."

Chapter 15

Steaming hot water swirled around Ming's body as he leaned back in a deep tub. The bathroom in the guest quarters of Chu On's mansion was a place he could spend his whole day. Chu On had ordered him to stay in the mansion since his work was finished, and Ming did not object.

His wounds had been dressed nicely, and he truly couldn't say another time where he physically felt so good. Around him were women wearing silk robes bathing him. They washed his hair and massaged his body in preparation for the ceremony to take place that evening. He kept trying to tell himself that he was ready, but the truth was he never thought about how he would feel when it really happened. "It" was becoming one of the most powerful men in China. Mentally he was all over the place. He was learning that taking his great-great-grandfather's place was more than just being the head of a powerful army. Chu On was also at the head of every underground ring there was and had politicians eating out of his pocket in fear. He would be inheriting all of that power. Ming was starting to wonder how he was going to handle all of that on top of the war still going on back in New York. How could he be in two places at once? He had always been the kind of person to work alone, but with all of the new things he was welcoming onto his plate, he knew he would need at least one other person at his side.

"You are tense," a soft voice said in his ear from behind him. "Is something wrong?"

It belonged to the woman who was giving him a shoulder massage with her delicate yet powerful fingers. He didn't answer her question. He didn't want to talk. She stopped massaging him to wave the other women away and out of the grand bathroom.

"Why did you make them leave?"

"So that you can release your worries in the presence of someone you can trust."

"The only person I trust is myself."

"If that is true, then I am sad for you," she said, resuming her massage.

"Forgive me if I'm apprehensive to relinquish my deepest thoughts to you." Sarcasm dripped from his voice.

"You say that because you have only just met me."

"Exactly. So why would you be somebody I trust?"

"Because my only purpose is to make you feel good. And if your mind is not at ease, mine cannot be either."

Her calm voice soothed Ming. Her words had gone directly through his strong exterior. He sighed.

"What worries you?" she asked again.

"This is all new to me. I feel like I know what I am doing, but at the same time I don't know. A person in my position is supposed to know it all the time." When Ming stopped talking, she giggled.

"Is that what you think a leader is? Because I have never known one to know exactly what he was doing all of the time. A good leader knows that it is wise to remain humble and teachable. Remember this: who you are has nothing to do with a title. It has everything to do with how you treat the people around you. When you are good to others, others are good to you. You can catch more flies with honey than with vinegar."

He let her words resonate and was shocked that he felt much better than he had seconds ago. She made who he was about to become seem as small as a breeze in the wind.

"How did you come to be so wise?"

"By remaining teachable," she said and stopped massaging him.

Before he could ask her why she stopped, he felt her stand up behind him. Seconds later, she got into the tub with him and was completely naked. It was the first time Ming had actually seen her face. She was a beautiful, slender woman. Her facial features were soft, and her lips were the color of a rose. They matched her cheeks. She had the most perky breasts he had ever seen, with succulent pink nipples. He let his eyes wander back up to her face and was met with a sly smile.

"Do you like what you see?"

"I should know your name before I answer that," he told her.

"Knowing my name won't change the fact that I am about to please you beyond your wildest dreams," she said, but when he didn't respond, she sighed softly. "It is Jia. My name is Jia."

"Jia, you have already helped me in more ways than you know. You do not need to add another."

"I know I do not need to, but I want to."

She submerged herself completely under the water and Ming's manly urges so badly wanted her to do what she was about to do. But the moment her lips touched his erect manhood, he pulled her back up. After wiping her wet hair from her face, she looked at him, confused. He could tell that she wasn't used to being denied, but those kinds of pleasantries weren't why he was in China. Ming was nowhere near a virgin, but he was such a disciplined man because sex did not rule him. It was not something he needed.

"I said you don't need to add another," Ming told her.

She nodded her head respectfully and snatched her robe from the floor. She kept her back to him when she removed herself from the tub. As she wrapped the robe around her, Ming could tell that he had embarrassed her. He opened his mouth to apologize, but there was a knock at the door right before it slid open. It was Hong. He looked from Jia to Ming and didn't bother to hide the amused expression on his face.

"I hope I'm not interrupting anything," he said with a smirk.

"Nothing at all," she snapped and then caught herself.

"Uh-huh." Hong raised a brow.

"As she said, you're not interrupting," Ming said. "She was just leaving."

Jia bowed her head respectfully at Hong as she passed. When she was gone, Ming grabbed a towel and wrapped it around his waist when he got out of the tub. He slid his feet into a pair of slippers and exited the bathroom.

"I see you're enjoying the perks of being the man already," Hong joked.

"I did not do anything with her. She bathed me, that's it."

"I'm not asking you to explain yourself, Ming. After tonight, if anybody does such a thing, it's a reason for their death. Speaking of which, that is why I came."

"Is something wrong?"

"Yes, very," Hong said, trying to feign a serious face. "You haven't decided on your attire for this evening."

Ming found himself grinning. He shrugged, mainly because he didn't really care. He wanted to get it all over with.

"It does not matter. Whatever is chosen for me is fine."

"Good, because I took the honor upon myself to pick," Hong said, motioning to the bed where he'd laid Ming's ceremonial robes.

"Red and gold like a phoenix," Ming said softly, thinking back to the story Chu On had told him.

"I felt these colors would be the most fitting."

"Thank you."

"Don't thank me yet. There is still much more that you need to know."

"Like what?"

"Like the people who aren't too happy that Chu On is naming you his successor and not someone else."

"Who would someone else be?"

"Our cousin Wei. He's big and ugly as hell. He has a strong following. And even some of our own seem to think that he would be more suited for the job than anyone else. He has worked closely with Chu On for years, and, no offense, but he definitely knows more about ruling than you."

"Then why did Chu On choose me over him?"

"Either because he saw something in you that he didn't see in him, or he knows his time is running short. Either way, Chu On did not want Wei as his successor. He told me in private that he truly feels that the Triad would go into flames if Wei ruled the underground trade. There has to be a certain order, and Wei has always been so power hungry."

"Do you think he will accept me as his leader?"

"He won't have a choice. You both share the same bloodline, but neither has more right to the throne than the other, which is why it is only Chu On's choice that matters. All power and ownership of everything will fall to you. You are about to have wealth beyond your greatest wishes. Now I will leave you to get dressed. When I come back, I will take you down to the ceremony."

As he was leaving, Ming fingered the silky-smooth fabric of his robes. There were rubies and yellow diamonds embroidered in them. A question suddenly came to his mind, and he turned to catch Hong before he left.

"Wait," he said.

"Yes, Ming?"

"Why were you not an option?"

"I have never been one to want so much power. I couldn't even imagine it. But still, I am loyal to it and would give my life for it," Hong explained.

"I'm . . . I'm going to need help. This is a new journey."

"It is for all of us."

"Will you stand beside me?"

"I'm glad you asked," Hong said with a wink. "But you never had to."

With that he was gone.

The walkway before Ming was lined with lit candles on each side. He stood at the start of the long cobblestone walkway watching the *Dance of the Phoenix* being performed by professional dancers. They threw lit torches in the air and caught them while moving their bodies to the music playing loudly. The crowd of at least a thousand lined up on the sides cheered them on. Ming found himself smiling at a small group of children trying to emulate what they saw.

When the dancers were done, they were replaced by actors who reenacted the story of Zianzo. It was all so breathtaking. Ming didn't know what to expect, but it wasn't that. Chu On sat on the far end of the walkway and smiled down at him. He seemed cheerful, a look Ming had never seen him wear.

"This is all for you," Hong whispered beside him. "Have you ever seen anything so great?"

"Never," Ming said, looking around. "Who are all these people Chu On invited onto his property?"

"Members of the Triad and family," Hong told him. "This isn't even half."

"Wow," Ming said, smiling back at everyone who was smiling at him.

It seemed unreal. However, the smile on his face fell when he noticed a group of men looking at him with malice written all over their faces.

"That's Wei and the ones closest to him," Hong told him, noticing the looks of contempt.

"Are they all Triad?"

"Yes." Hong nodded.

"I thought you said they would accept me."

"I never said they would be happy about it." Hong grinned and patted him on the shoulder. "Don't pay them any mind. Look. It's time."

A gong sounded loudly, and all noise stopped. The performers bowed and moved off of the walkway into the crowds of people. Chu On stood up from his seat and surveyed the host of people and put his arms in the air. He began speaking in Chinese, but Ming's mind translated it.

"We are gathered here today to honor a great transition. I have done many great things in my life, but now it is time to give someone else the chance to lead and to experience this world of wonder. I know I have made the most honorable choice to put all of my trust in my great-great-grandson, Ming Chen. You will follow him. And through love or fear you will obey him. This is my decree."

"And it shall be followed," the crowd said back in unison.

The gong sounded again, and Chu On motioned for Ming to step forward. He did, with Hong still at his side. Ming walked with his head held high. Whispers from the crowd blew his way in the wind, but he paid them no mind. As he walked, he saw Jia standing in the crowd. She looked away from him when he passed. When they reached Chu On, Hong bowed and stepped to the side with other Triad members to watch the transfer take place. Ming dropped to his knees when Chu On approached him and looked into his face.

"Ming Chen, do you humbly accept the responsibility I am bestowing upon you?"

"Yes. I do."

"Then it is time I pass everything on," Chu On said and removed the diamond-encrusted jade pendant from his robes. He then attached it to Ming's. "Everything you need is within this pendant. Always remember that. To your feet."

Ming stood up, and Chu On turned him to face the crowd. What Ming saw staring back at him was not just an army. They were family. They looked at him with awe in their eyes, and one by one, they bowed.

"The new leader of the Triad! Ming Ch—"

He stopped talking abruptly, and Ming turned to see why. He stared horrified at the perfect red circle in the center of Chu On's forehead. Ming caught him before he fell dead to the floor.

"Nooo!" Hong shouted and drew his weapon. "Protect Ming!"

Ming suddenly was circled by men who all had their weapons drawn. They were ready to give their lives for him and did. They began dropping like flies around him. No gunshots were heard, and Ming didn't know if that was because of a silencer or because of all the screaming. He surveyed the crowd, and his eyes stopped when he spotted Wei. He and his followers had their guns out, and they were pointed at Ming.

"Hong, there!"

Hong looked to where Ming was pointing. Wei saw that he had been spotted and smiled big at them. He stood up on a fountain and looked Ming in the eyes.

"Look at him cowering! That is no leader!" he shouted to the people who hadn't run away. "I am your true leader!"

"Do not believe a word he says. He murdered Chu On!" Hong shouted back. "That is treason!"

"I saved us from an old man who in his haste was about to make an outsider our leader."

"Ming is no outsider. He is family!"

"How many times has he even come to China? He knows nothing about our people and our customs. He is an American!"

"He is the man Chu On chose to lead us! And I will follow him." Hong poked his chest out.

"I won't! And anyone else who does will die at my hand. Join me now or die!"

Wei looked around at the other members of the Triad and challenged them with his gaze. Surprisingly, a handful went to stand with him and his followers. Not only did they stand with him, but they pointed their weapons at Ming. Hong's eyes widened when he saw how many would disrespect Chu On's ruling. But Ming wasn't surprised. He'd seen people turn for much less. He stared into Chu On's face and couldn't help but to wonder if that was his fate. He had ruled with an iron fist, and it was the same fist that had ended him. He'd told Ming that he would rule with guidance, and at that moment Jia's voice flooded his mind.

"You can catch more flies with honey than vinegar."

She was right, but right then he didn't have any honey or vinegar. He had a loaded gun. He used his fingers to close Chu On's eyes and stood slowly to his feet. Wei was too busy selling himself to the people to notice Ming drawing his weapon. Ming extended his arm, casually pushing Hong's head to the side. He fired the gun twice, feeling the recoil in his forearm. The men standing by Wei jumped as Ming's bullets tore his face off and made him fly off of the fountain. His body lay dead in the grass, and silence filled the air. Slowly, every weapon pointed at

Ming lowered. Some of Wei's followers and his would-be followers ran. But the ones who stayed dropped to their knees and began begging for forgiveness.

"Now I am your only leader," Ming shouted for them all to hear.

Chapter 16

A cold chill from a high-velocity fan hit Zo when he walked into one of his warehouses. He was going around checking up on things and overseeing that all backed-up orders were being shipped out. The last thing he wanted was another Jahmar coming out of the wood works. He wanted to keep all of his customers happy.

Zo was pleased to see that there wasn't a still body in sight. Even with all of the freight boxes stacked around, there was room for everyone to bustle around and get their jobs done. It smelled like cedar, and Zo could hear the machinery going in the back. Sometimes they had to make their own shipment containers to fulfill orders. Zo was happy that everyone was making good use of their time. He got the attention of a man named Martin as he passed.

"How is everything coming along?" Zo asked.

"What's up, boss!" Martin greeted him. "So far so good. A few of the trucks are running late, but we should still be able to get everything out by the end of the day."

"Perfect. How is inventory looking?"

"Demand is picking up again, but we should be good for another two months before we need to restock again. No one is asking for anything crazy so far."

"Good," Zo said even though that wasn't how he felt.

Louisa had made things very loud and clear that she would not supply him anymore unless he came to Florida. She had put him in a very delicate position. Even with everything she showed them that Florida had to offer, it didn't compare to home. He didn't want to leave. He wanted to help Boogie rebuild what had fallen.

"Is everything okay, boss?" Martin asked, interrupting his thoughts.

"Why wouldn't they be?" Zo wondered if the unease he felt showed on his face.

"It's just"—Martin looked around and lowered his voice—"a lot of us heard about Eduardo. I still can't believe he would do something like that. Not after everything Marco did for him."

"Well, he did. And if you heard about what he did, then you heard about what happened to him too, eh?" Zo asked, and Martin nodded his head slowly. "Good. That or worse will be anyone else's fate who chooses to betray me. Now get back to work."

Martin hurried along and left Zo to continue his walk around. The warehouse was filled with crates, like it always was. He tried not to think about what would happen once it all cleared out. As long as he had breath in his body, it wouldn't.

"Zo!"

He groaned loudly when he heard his sister's voice. He had been trying hard to avoid her ever since they got back home. And that included staying in his condo instead of the family house and ignoring her phone calls. He didn't even know how she had found him. There were at least five other warehouses that she could have checked before that one. He could have acted like he didn't hear her, but there were entirely too many firearms in arm's reach of her.

"What, Daniella?" He turned and faced her irritated face.

"Don't 'what, Daniella' me like I've already gotten on your nerves," she snapped. "You've been avoiding me, why?"

"I haven't been avoiding you," Zo lied.

"Lorenzo, I've known you my entire life. I know when you're lying to me. You've been acting weird since we got back from Florida."

"Have I?"

"Yes! Does it have anything to do with Florida?" she asked, and Zo didn't say anything. "You don't want to go, do you?"

"Is it obvious?" He began to walk away from her. As he passed one of his workers, he took a clipboard from him and checked it. It said, "Strawberry inventory," and he knew that meant grenades. He shook his head before giving the clipboard back. "Take that extra one hundred off of this order. We have a higher demand for things this month, and we need all of our inventory."

"Yes, sir," the man said and walked away.

"You're worried, aren't you?" Daniella caught up to him, not wanting to let the topic go.

"I am never worried."

"You should learn to lie better."

"I don't know what you want me to say, Daniella."

"Something! You know like I know that time is winding down. You only have a week to give Louisa an answer. Have you even told Mama about Louisa?"

"You know I haven't. You heard her. Mama doesn't like her. And there is no point in telling her because a week is still enough time to find another supplier."

"You heard what Louisa said. Her reach is far, and we probably won't be able to find another supplier who doesn't get their weapons from her."

"Exactly. That's what she *said*. People will say anything when they're trying to get something from you. I have to try."

"Or . . . you can just do what she wants."

"What did you just say?" Zo stopped walking.

"You heard what I said. No need to repeat it."

"Why would you ever think I'd do that?"

"Because maybe it's the best thing for us. You see Papa was going to take the deal."

"Papa isn't here to explain his side of the story. You don't think it's strange at all everything that she's saying? I mean, we *knew* him."

"Did we really? You saw the proof just like I did."

"I don't know. Something just isn't sitting right in my gut. And Papa always told me to follow it. I mean, why go through all of this trouble just to get us in Florida? She doesn't even know us."

"We are family. And blood is bond."

"If you say so."

"So what are you going to do then? Ask your precious Boogie for help?"

"Yes, that's exactly what I'm going to do. We're trying to rebuild. All the shit Papa left me in Florida you can have or I'm going to sell it. I don't want it. Things were fine before. I can't just walk away from Queens now to go play kingdom with someone I don't know or trust."

"Papa—"

"Papa lived a good life here. He built here. These were the makings of him. I will not let it go so easily. Mama has been through enough. I won't just leave her, nor will I uproot her. The others and me . . . we'll find a way."

"I can't believe you. You want to fall into the same cycle that got Papa killed!"

"If we leave, what about everybody else? Huh?" Zo snapped back. "I loved the man, but if what Louisa is saying is true—"

"It is!"

"*If* it is true, Papa was going to make a selfish decision and say fuck everybody else. These people have worked for him and been loyal for years. I won't just let the well run dry for them to save my own ass!"

"Well, Papa—"

"I'm not him!"

"I know. You remind me of that every day just by looking at you," she sneered. "You really want to take this risk by trying to pull a rabbit out of a magician's hat? Louisa—"

"Louisa what? Is a dangerous woman? The only thing she has over me is that she is my supplier. If she wants to go, she can go. You can join her if you like. It seems like that's what you want to do anyway."

"Maybe I will."

Daniella turned on her heels and left him in the dust. He clenched his jaw as he watched her walk away. He wanted to call her back, but he didn't. Neither of them were in a position where they could talk clearly. Instead, he went back to overlooking the orders being sent out.

Chapter 17

There was only supposed to be one ceremony in Ming's time in China, but it quickly turned into two. He refused to leave until after Chu On's funeral. There were three days of visitation with his family before he was finally put to rest. Even after that, however, it was hard for Ming to leave. Chu On's death made way for much chaos to break out in the streets of Hong Kong. When it was learned that one of the Triad's own members was responsible for killing Chu On, it caused much discord. There was no balance, and Ming felt he needed to be there to put everything back together. With the great power he'd been bestowed came a great responsibility. But that didn't change the fact that there was a slate in New York that needed to be wiped clean. He promised Hong he would be back soon and entrusted him with the responsibility of keeping things in as much order as he could.

Other jets were landing on the runway when Ming stepped off his. He stretched his arms wide, trying to loosen up his stiff body. Although the sun wasn't shining brightly, he put on a pair of sunglasses, yawning as he walked down the steps. He took a deep breath of New York air when he descended the final two steps. He hadn't been back to his family's mansion since he killed his father. In fact, he hadn't even thought about what he had done since he left. It was his hand that slayed Tao, and he didn't feel anything at the time. He still felt nothing. No sadness, no regret . . . nothing. Not even when he looked his mother in the eyes. Maybe it was because Tao stopped being his father long ago. He had been his boss, and Ming realized right before he pulled the trigger that he hated having a boss. Stringing Tao's body up for everyone to see had been Chu On's idea.

Ming wished he could have more time with Chu On. He seemed to be the perfect balance of good and evil. Ming had killed so much in his father's name and done so much of his bidding that he wondered if there was still any good left inside of him. He shook the thought away as he went to the all-white SUV waiting to take him home. The first thing he was going to do was meditate to get his body used to the time change. He got inside and waited for his driver, Peng, to greet him, which he always did. But that time he didn't. It was strange, but Ming was too tired to care.

"Take me home," he said.

Peng still didn't speak. He just nodded his head and pulled out of the runway. Ming laid his head back on the seat and rolled the window down some so he could smell the air of New York. He let his body relax and just took in the scenery. He had to admit he missed it. Before he knew it, he had dozed off.

Ming didn't know how long he had been asleep when he felt something cold tapping on his temple. He opened his eyes and sat up, startled. His door was open, and they had stopped in an abandoned lot. And staring into his face was the same black man who had knocked him out before. The man was pointing a chrome pistol in his face and chewing a piece of gum.

"You!" Ming exclaimed.

"Y'all ain't got manners in China? I have a name. It's Nathan."

"I do not care what your name is. Where is my driver? Where is Peng?"

"You're lookin' at him," Nathan said with a grin.

Ming took the time to actually look at Nathan, who was wearing Peng's driver uniform. He had been the one who had picked him up from the airport. How could he have been so stupid?

"Where is my driver?"

"Alive, that's all you need to know," Nathan said as a black SUV pulled beside them. "Look, our ride is here."

"I'm not going anywhere with you!" Ming said and reached for his waist but felt nothing.

"I disarmed you while you were sleepin'. Now are you gon' come the easy way, or do I have to kick your ass again?"

"Where are you taking me?"

"The heads of the other four families want to have a chat with you. Without any troops bein' involved."

"So what do you call yourself?"

"I'm just here to get you there."

"And if I refuse?"

"I kick your ass and make you come," Nathan said and held up a pair of handcuffs.

Ming looked at the gun in his hand and then glared at him. Without saying anything else, he held his arms out. Once the cuffs were on, he got in the back of the other vehicle, and a black cloth bag was placed over his head.

After Nathan called and said he had the package, Boogie felt like he was checking his Rolex every five minutes. He entrusted Nathan with bringing Ming to the Five Families' meeting place because he had taken him down before. But still, with the luck he'd had, he was well aware that anything could happen. When he wasn't checking his watch, he was tapping the round table.

"Boogie, relax. They'll be here," Morgan said, noticing how antsy he was.

"And before they arrive, let's get a few things clear," Nicky's voice sounded, and he leaned into the table. "This is going to be a civilized meeting. Nobody is to make a move on anyone. Treat this place as sacred ground as the ones before us did."

"Way to sound Jedi," Morgan teased.

"This is serious, Morgan. Some of us were affected more by the rampage of the Chinese than others." Nicky let his eyes go from Zo to Boogie. "Remember that it wasn't Ming's hand that killed Marco or that shot Roz."

"I'll try," Zo said.

"I need you to do more than try," Nicky said sternly. "What about you, Boogie? Will you be good to go when you see Ming?"

"I'll be straight."

"All right. Remember that the goal for this meeting is a peaceful resolve. Loss and hurt don't just belong to any one of us. We all experienced that shit. And, Boogie, I know you've done a lot to right your wrongs, but this will be the time it counts the most."

"Roger that."

"Good."

A total of forty-five minutes passed before there was finally a knock on the door. Morgan got up to open it, and Nathan stepped through. With him was who Boogie could only assume was Ming. His wrists were cuffed, and he had a bag over his head.

"Why the bag?" Boogie asked after Ming was seated in what once had been Li's chair.

"For effect." Nathan shrugged and removed the bag from over Ming's head.

Boogie watched as he blinked and let his eyes readjust to the light. When they did, Ming took in his surroundings and the people inside of the room. He didn't look happy to see them.

"His gun and other weapons?" Boogie asked.

"In the car."

"Good. You can take those cuffs off him."

"You sure? This motherfucka might not look like much, but he got some hands on him."

"We're not here to fight," Morgan chimed in. "You can take them off."

"A'ight. But I'll be right outside if you need me."

Nathan removed the handcuffs and left the room, closing the door behind him.

"We're glad you could make it, Ming," Nicky said, breaking the ice.

"Did I have much of a choice?"

"We wish we didn't have to go through such lengthy measures to get you here, but we needed you alone."

"And how did you know that I would be at the airport?"

"Maybe not everyone on your side is happy with the way things have been goin' either," Boogie said.

"You of all people speak about the way things are going? The same man who killed my great-uncle?"

"With the help of your father," Boogie rebutted. "He's the one who told me where Li would be that night."

"Your father also murdered mine." Zo's voice was cold as he talked. "And then he tried to kill Caesar."

"Yeah, so it's back on you, buddy," Boogie said.

"We aren't here to point the finger or play the blame game," Nicky spoke before Ming could. "We all have played a part in this war."

"Well . . ." Morgan said, but Nicky shot her a look that silenced her.

"None of our hands are clean. Boogie and I can sit at the same table peacefully even though at one point we wanted each other dead. Why? Because we see the bigger picture. And we need you to see it too, Ming."

"The bigger picture," Ming scoffed at Nicky. "And what exactly would that be?"

"The pact kept peace for years until things turned bad." Nicky looked to everyone in the room. "I think we should put it back into place but make it our own. We have all lost money in this war. And not only that, but outsiders have invaded our home because we look weak to them, fighting each other. Yes, we are five families, but when shit like that happens, we should turn into one. The reason why people fall from the top in other places is because they get greedy. We have survived for so long because we have always been willing to share. There shouldn't be one family who controls everything. And I think we all know why."

"There is no balance. Just constant war," Zo said.

"Exactly. My uncle put a stop to that when he was around our age. And we can do it again today. We have to end the feuding. I call for a cease-fire and a truce. What do you say, Ming?"

Silence overcame the room, and all eyes went to Ming. His face held no real expression. He just looked . . . bored. Like nothing Nicky said had resonated. Finally, after a long minute passed, he spoke.

"I say that was a nice speech. But I know you only say all of this because of fear." Ming's voice was icy. "I'm sure you know that I have come into an army of thousands. You know that if I continue to fight, I will win. And that means I will have majority control over the five boroughs. It would be so easy even if you all fought me together."

"See? I knew this would be a waste of time," Zo said in frustration.

"You have not let me finish," Ming said to him, and suddenly his tone softened. "Too much recently have I seen what stolen power does to a man. And not only to him, but all of the people around him. It changes them, not for the better. That path always leads to death. I have done many things, but so far none have turned my soul black. And I fear that continuing a war here would. I will tell my people that the feud between my family and yours is over."

"And why should we believe you?" Zo asked.

"Because I now have more important things to focus my attention on. But even if I didn't, I never wanted the same things as my father and my uncle."

"Is that why you killed Tao?" Boogie asked.

"I didn't think you would be so sentimental about his death," Ming said to him. "But no, I killed him because he was in the way."

"All to get an army."

"If that is what you would like to believe. There was no other way to tame him besides sending him to the afterlife. I do not need you to understand."

Nobody said anything for a while. Ming's words were absent of emotion. He spoke about killing his own father the same way a person would describe killing a bug. Boogie couldn't imagine the pain Tao had inflicted on Ming, but it had turned him into a cold-blooded killer. Nicky was the one to break the ice.

"That's your business. As long as his death isn't pinned on any of us, we are squared away on it. So what terms can we come to an agreement on?"

"Like I said, I don't want what my father or my uncle Li wanted. However, I don't want the same things as you either. I do not wish to be a part of any new pact that you put together. I will tell my people that the feud between my family and all of yours is over. But I will not come back to join you."

"What exactly does that mean?" Boogie asked.

"It means that you continue doing business with each other like the Bronx doesn't exist. I stay out of your way, and you stay out of mine."

It wasn't exactly what they were going for, and Boogie found himself clenching his jaw. He looked at Nicky, who seemed to be lost in his own deep thoughts. Zo's head was rested on his clasped hands, and Morgan just looked shocked.

"I guess . . . I guess this is the best deal we're gon' get from you, huh?" Boogie sighed. "What y'all think?"

"I think we accept," Nicky said, and the others agreed.

"Good," Ming told them. "Can I leave now?"

Boogie nodded his head, and Ming bowed to them. They all watched him stand up and leave. Nathan walked back in the room and pointed a thumb in Ming's direction.

"Y'all just lettin' him go like that?"

"We came to an agreement," Nicky said and sighed. "The Bronx is exiled from us and us from it. Put the word out."

Zo had parked next to Boogie in the parking garage, so the two left the meeting together. It felt strange not to be escorted out by their entourage, but they didn't want Ming to feel intimidated. So they all showed up naked. No shooters, no guards. Nothing. It was a dangerous thing to do for anyone of their caliber, but it was to show good faith. And in the end, they got something good out of it. As long as Ming held up his end of the bargain.

"Crazy shit, huh?" Boogie asked when they got to their vehicles.

"Yeah. I don't know what I expected, but it damn sure wasn't that. Do you believe him?"

"I don't know. I guess we just have to see. For some reason though, I think he might be for real. He looked—"

"Bored?"

"Nah. Tired. I think we're all tired. But now, hopefully, things can go back to normal."

Zo wished he could share Boogie's smile. He couldn't, though. He still hadn't found another weapons supplier. It seemed as though Louisa had been telling the truth about having a long reach. Zo couldn't get anyone to answer his calls, let alone set up a meeting. His troubled expression didn't go unnoticed by Boogie.

"Yo, you good, Zo?"

"Nah . . . I'm not actually. I don't know if things are actually gonna go back to normal on my end," he said with a sigh.

He then went on to tell Boogie all about what was going on. And how he had less than five days to give Louisa an answer or he would be on ice. To his surprise, Boogie didn't return his worry.

"I wish you had told me about this shit a long time ago," he said.

"I know, amigo. But shit has just been so fucked up all around."

"I understand. And I can tell you the reason nobody is answerin' your calls."

"Why?"

"Because you're tryin'a fuck with them suit-and-tie motherfuckas when everything you need is in the hood. Listen, I'm gon' link you with Gino's people, and I guarantee they'll get you anything you need. I heard there's been a drought that way since he died anyway."

"Yo, Boogie. You're a lifesaver."

"We family, man," Boogie said and slapped hands with him. "I'm gon' head out though. You be safe out there."

"No doubt," Zo said, feeling a ton lighter.

Zo got inside his car to drive off, never knowing that his every move was being watched.

Chapter 18

Boogie and Zo never paid attention to the black BMW with the tinted windows parked five spaces away, but they should have. The driver's side window was cracked just enough that Louisa could hear everything that the two men said. She'd spent the day following Zo around undetected, hoping to learn something that would make him join her sooner. But what she found out in the parking garage was that he'd already made his decision. He was proving to be more difficult than Marco. With him at least she was able to weaponize his guilt against him for staying away from her so long. But Zo didn't know her from a can of paint which meant there was no loyalty.

She glared at the one Zo called Boogie, and everything about him put her in the mindset of Caesar. She could tell he and Zo were more than just business partners. They were friends. No, they were more than friends. They were family.

Family. There was that word again. It was the only thing she never had. Not really. When her mother died and she had to go live with her papa, she always felt like the outsider. Her stepmother never loved her like a daughter. It hurt, especially since she didn't have her own mama there. So Louisa watched her siblings get love and attention that she desperately wanted. It drove her crazy. Her papa tried to connect with her on outings with just them, but all it reminded Louisa of was that she was not really part of the family. The only one who didn't make her feel like that was Marco. So he was the only one in the house she spared. She began to play horrible tricks on everyone except him. The last straw was when she put bleach in her stepmother's shampoo and soap. She had to be hospitalized. Louisa had never felt so much joy in her life. But it was what made her papa send her away to boarding school. And when she graduated, they still didn't want anything to do with her. All but Marco turned their backs on her. But then he had to go and let his wife ruin their relationship and keep her niece and nephew away from her. Now there was Lorenzo, turning his back on her just like everyone else before him.

That made Louisa's blood boil. She was Zo's real family, not Boogie. But she had to admit, he must have been something big if he could do for Zo what Louisa was sure nobody would. And that was a problem. He was a problem.

When she traveled to New York, she had imagined more chaos than what she had witnessed. It was the reason she had approached Marco in the first place, because the Five Families were in disarray. Louisa always wanted Marco at her side but feared making a move on him before. When the five boroughs worked harmoniously together, they were powerful, too powerful. Louisa wouldn't have stood a chance. Not only that, but she didn't want to bring unwanted attention to her operation. So she kept providing Marco with whatever he needed. But the moment she heard that things were going to shit with Marco's little club, she swarmed him. It wasn't easy to persuade him to leave it all behind. He had built an entire empire and was so hell-bent on helping Caesar with whatever the leader of the boy band needed help with. But when two of the five family heads died, he agreed. Marco told her that there were a few loose ends to tie up, but then he was willing to pass the torch and start fresh, with his immediate family in tow of course. Louisa wasn't too thrilled about his wife, Christina, coming with him. The last time the two women saw each other, it wasn't a pretty sight. But it was a small price to pay to get what she had always wanted.

She still planned on getting what she wanted. There were just a few . . . bumps in the road she had to take care of first. Boogie was one of them. She had to get him out of Zo's life for good.

Chapter 19

"Man, these niggas are weak! What the fuck was that?"

Bentley almost threw his PlayStation headset across the room. He was playing *Call of Duty* and getting frustrated because every time he respawned, he got killed again. He felt like the game was cheating him, and his team wasn't showing up. He knew the best thing for him to do was to just get off it before he broke his PS5.

He turned it off and went into the kitchen to fix himself something to drink. Grabbing his phone from the counter, he checked it for any missed calls. He thought Boogie would have returned his calls by then, given the fact that he wouldn't let Bentley ride with him that morning. He thought it was crazy that Boogie was going to the meeting naked with no shooters around him. But then again if Nicky, Zo, and even Morgan were there, he wasn't really alone. Bentley had tried playing the game to calm his nerves, but that didn't do anything but make them worse. Maybe no news was good news, especially since the meeting should have been over by then. It was coming up on one in the afternoon. Ming's plane had landed that morning.

Although Boogie hadn't called him, he did have a missed call from Roz. He couldn't express how good it felt to see her name pop up on his phone. He poured himself a glass of Hennessy on the rocks and called her back.

"Hello?" she answered on the first ring.

"What's up, Roz, how you feelin'?"

"Good. I would have been feeling better if you had answered when I called you. Being on bed rest is so boring, and your niece is tearing up this man's house!"

Bentley found himself cracking up. He was imagining his niece running around Caesar's, destroying everything in sight. Caesar was a rich man, though. He could replace anything she broke.

"Anyways, I can't do nothing but watch movies. I was calling you to ask you the name of that movie we used to watch when we were younger."

"What was it about?"

"Nigga, I don't know. Can't you read my mind?"

"Roz . . ."

"Fine, fine. It had a llama in it."

"*The Emperor's New Groove*," Bentley answered, knowing instantly what she was talking about.

"That's it! Thank you."

"No problem. But on a serious note, how are you feelin'? Getting shot ain't no joke."

"My wound is healing up nicely, and I'm getting my energy back every day. I just miss my own room. And my own stuff, you know? Don't get me wrong, I'm thankful to Caesar for letting us stay here, but I still don't know why I can't rest up at home."

Bentley had to think fast. Boogie hadn't told her that their home had been burned down. Eventually she would find out, but he wouldn't be the one to tell her either.

"The streets are still a little hot. Boogie just wants you in the safest place for you. And I can't blame him."

"Whose side are you on?" Roz whined.

"Always yours, and that's why I have to agree with Boogie on this one."

"Uh-huh. Speaking of him, have you talked to him recently?"

"I've been waitin' on him to hit me today. Why, what's up?" Bentley asked and sipped his Hennessey.

He made a hissing sound when it hit his chest. He always joked and said that was how he knew it was working. Roz grew quiet on the other end. He was about to repeat his question, but her voice sounded again.

"Did he tell you what happened at the—"

Knock! Knock!

The knock at his door drowned out what she said next. He wasn't expecting company, and Boogie usually called before he showed up. Same with Tazz. But who else could it be?

"Sis, let me call you back," he said and hung up the phone. He placed the device down but kept his drink in his hand when he went to answer the door. "Who is it?

"Morgan. So open the door."

Bentley still checked the peephole. When he saw her, he stepped back and smoothed down his shirt real quick before opening the door. Morgan stood there looking fine as always. That day, she rocked her hair in wild curls all over her head. She had on a fur coat and skinny jeans so tight they looked like skin. Her cheekbones rose, and she saw him, and he stepped out of the way so that she had room to walk through.

"Morgan? I wasn't expectin' you."

"I guess that's because I didn't call first. My bad. I hope it's not a problem."

"Nah, no worries. I actually thought you were Boogie for a second."

"He didn't call you?" Morgan asked, surprised.

"Same thing I was thinking. But if you're here, I assume the meeting didn't go too bad."

"It didn't go bad at all, actually. The Chinese are going to stand down."

"Just like that?"

"That's what Ming told us. We have to let him show and prove, I guess. That's not all he said, though. He admitted to killing his own father."

"'Cause that nigga was crazy!" Bentley blurted out. "I don't care what motherfuckas say about Boogie. He ain't have shit on Tao."

"I agree. Especially knowing that he's the one who set Li up to be killed."

"Like I said, crazy! So Ming just gon' start his own shit up in the BX like Bosco did in Staten Island?"

"I don't know. He said he has other things on his plate. So I hope they keep him busy for a long time. I don't even want to think about another feud. I just want to make some money."

"Word. Is that what you came here to tell me?"

"That and . . ." Morgan walked to an outlet in his living room with a charger hanging from it. "I left my charger over here when I was babysitting Amber."

"You makin' paper, girl. You mean to tell me you really came all this way just to grab a charger? You could've just gone and bought a new one."

"Just because you have money doesn't mean you have to spend it."

"Wise words."

"Uh-huh. Plus, maybe I just wanted to see you."

"Is that why you wore them tight-ass jeans?"

"Boy!" Morgan laughed and tossed one of the couch's decorative pillows in his direction. "My jeans are not that tight."

"I mean, it's not a bad thing. I'm not complainin'."

"I bet you aren't. Anyway, what were you doing before I got here?"

"Shit. Just on the game. Waitin' on Boogie to hit me up."

"What game do you like to play?"

"*Call of Duty*. You know, killin' niggas."

"Stop. You were probably the one getting killed," she teased.

"Now I see it's you who got jokes. You want a drink."

"Maybe, depends on what you're drinking."

"Hennessy on the rocks," Bentley answered, and she made a face.

"I guess I'll have a little."

He got up and went into the kitchen. When he came back, he had another glass of brown liquor in his hand. He sat down and handed it to her.

"You must not be too fond of the dark shit. You're probably the type who's ready to whoop a nigga's ass off the Hen, huh?"

"Can you stop?" Morgan was able to get out through her laughter.

"What? I'm just tryin'a figure out if I'ma need to take cover here soon."

"If it ever gets to that point, you might want to. Diana has me training twice a week with professional fighters."

"That's what's up. I know Diana is your mom and all, but I think it's dope how she's really taking you under her wing."

"It is. I just wish she wouldn't worry about me so much. Boogie is running two boroughs, Caesar is letting Nicky do his thing, but here I am with training wheels on."

"In her defense, she's never gon' stop worryin' about you. It's in a mother's nature. You just have to keep showin' her that you're capable. Like you did with Stefano in Staten Island."

They sat next to each other on the couch with their drinks. As Bentley continued to sip, he noticed Morgan eyeing him. Like *eyeing him*. He was a little buzzed, so he found himself grinning.

"What you looking at, girl?"

"You," she said flirtatiously, letting him know he wasn't the only one feeling the effects of the Hennessy.

"Is that right?"

"Mm-hmm. You know, Boogie seems to think that you like me."

"What do you think?"

"I think I see you checking me out all the time, but you act like you're too scared to speak on what you feel."

"Trust me, I ain't never scared."

"Prove it then," she said and removed her coat.

Under it, she revealed, she was wearing a low-cut bodysuit. Her erect nipples were staring right at him, begging him to put them in his mouth. Bentley couldn't lie. He was completely caught off guard. One, she was Boogie's sister. And two, quiet as kept, he had fantasized about what her kitty would feel like wrapped around him more times that he could count. He instantly felt his erection grow until he was rock hard.

"Are you sure? I mean, I was thinking we should start with dinner and a movie."

"Bentley, I am grown. We can do that shit any other time. But right now you're here. I'm here . . . and I want you to make love to me. I mean, I need to sample the goods before I let you wife me."

"You think I can't please you?"

"I'm just trying to make sure," she said and pulled her breasts out.

She pinched one and licked the other while looking him in the eye. She was a freak. And that was fine, because he was one too.

"I'll take that as a challenge," he told her.

He didn't need another invitation. Before he knew it, his lips were pressed on hers, and their tongues were swimming in each other's mouths.

Chapter 20

The sounds of a vihuela accompanied a woman singing a beautiful song in Spanish to a bar crowd. The lighting inside was dim, and everyone seemed to be having a good time. Louisa found herself being envious of their laughter from where she sat in the back sipping a martini. She was dressed in a black dress that made it easy for her to blend in with the shadows. A buzz overcame her, and she found herself swaying to the sound of the singer's voice.

"You seem to be enjoying yourself," a voice said, approaching the table. "I was surprised when you called and told me that you were here."

"Thank you for coming, Daniella." Louisa smiled up into her niece's face. "Please, sit."

Daniella looked at the seat across from her and hesitated. Louisa read her like a book. She could tell the girl was apprehensive about meeting with her, but there she was, wearing a formfitting black and silver jumpsuit at that. She hadn't gotten dressed and done her makeup for no reason, and Louisa knew there was no way she was just going to leave.

"Sit," she said again, and finally Daniella did.

"What do you want?"

"I can't just want to see you? You and your brother left Florida so quickly."

"That's because we saw more than we needed to."

"Well, what did you think?"

"I think it's crazy to believe you know someone. Then they die and you find out that you were missing out of a big part of them."

"A big part that can be yours. Yours and Lorenzo's," Louisa said, but Daniella shook her head.

"If you're here to try to get me to talk my brother into agreeing to your deal, you might want to come up with a new game plan."

"And why do you say that?"

"Papa signed ownership of all his properties in Florida to Lorenzo. He plans on selling them all."

"What?" Louisa was in the middle of taking another sip of her martini but stopped the glass at her lips. "He's going to do what?"

"He doesn't want anything to do with Florida. He thinks he'll be able to find a new weapons supplier and that he won't need you."

"Is that so?" Louisa said and placed her drink on the table. She leaned forward and looked Daniella in the eyes. "What do you think about that?"

"It doesn't matter what I think," Daniella scoffed. "Lorenzo holds all of the power."

"That's not what I asked you. I asked you what you think about all of that. Your thoughts matter to me."

"I think . . ." Daniella paused like she was trying to think of the right words to say. In the midst of that, a bartender came to take her order. She ordered a strawberry margarita on the rocks and turned back to Louisa when the man walked away. "I think I'm ready for something new. New York is my home. I grew up in Queens because that's always where Papa was. But . . . it feels empty without him. I don't see why we can't do what we do here somewhere else."

"Exactly," Louisa said. "And in Florida you wouldn't just be capped at being weapons dealers. There would be a world of opportunity and a never-ending cashflow. This I can promise you. Daniella, I will be all the way honest with you. I did call you here in hopes that you could talk some sense into your brother, but now that you are here, I can't help but to be so thankful to be spending time with my *familia*."

She stopped talking and smiled into Daniella's pretty face. She saw a lot of Christina there, but she also saw so many hints of Marco. It made her happy to still be able to see him somewhere. Daniella's lips started to curl upward, but then they stopped, and a troubled look appeared in her eyes.

"Louisa, you said before that my *abuela* was unkind to you. How?"

Louisa's face grew stiff as thoughts of Kimberly Alverez flooded her mental. The hatred she felt for her had never left her heart. Kimberly was dead, but Louisa hoped with all of her heart that her contempt had traveled into the afterlife. Daniella, seeing Louisa's expression, put a hand up.

"I'm sorry. I didn't mean to bring up old trauma."

"No, it's okay. I just don't want to taint the memories you have of your grandmother with the ones I have of her. I'm sure she loved you. You were her family. But me? I wasn't. I was just a burden."

"I'm sorry you felt like that."

"Mmm, don't apologize for something you didn't do. But I hope you understand why it was so important to me that we have a close relationship."

"Is that really the only reason you want us to come? Because we are family?"

"Yes. I may look fabulous, but I realize my mortal life is getting shorter and shorter by the day. What I have built I don't want to go into the hands of anybody else. What DeMarco has built here is beautiful, but it is nothing like what I have. He didn't pass down an empire to Lorenzo. He passed him a fraction of one."

"Do you have any kids?"

"No. I never had any," Louisa answered sadly. "But maybe one day you can take over for me the way Lorenzo took over for your father."

"Really?" Daniella's eyes lit up like a Christmas tree.

"Really. I would love to groom you, Daniella."

"Groom . . . me?"

"Yes. I could tell from the moment I met you that you have the same fire inside of you that I did when I first started."

"Papa used to only let me handle the numbers, nothing more and nothing less."

"We all start somewhere."

"How did you? Start I mean?" Daniella asked.

"I was fucking a very rich man at the time."

"What?" Daniella asked with a laugh.

Louisa laughed too. At that moment, the bartender returned with Daniella's drink. Before he left, he placed some extra drinks and salt down on the table.

"It's true," Louisa said. "He was a criminal mastermind who I'll just call Charming for now. Charming smuggled weapons into America from overseas and sold them at a higher price. I paid attention, and when he died, I took over for him."

"Died?"

"He had a very unfortunate accident. It left me devastated, but just as he took care of me in life, he did in death. With the remainder of his inventory and his connections, I went into business for myself. Your father was my very first customer, and I guess you can say I just grew from there into the boss I am today."

"Wow, I want to be like you when I grow up!" Daniella said.

"And if you join me, you will. We will be much stronger together. But first, I need something from you."

"Yes?"

"Can you tell me everything you know about someone named Boogie?"

Chapter 21

As usual, the Sugar Trap was jumping on a Friday evening. The girls were doing their thing, and it was a packed house. The girls were doing what they did best: filling the men up with liquor and emptying their pockets. Diana moved in the shadows, watching and making sure nothing was amiss. Her eyes fell on two of the girls on stage. One of them was a new girl who called herself Phoenix. She was twirling on a pole with one of the OGs, Waterfall. She chose that name because she always had a long blue weave in and her body moved as fluid as a waterfall. There had to have been thousands of dollars thrown on the stage, which Diana let them keep as long as they paid their weekly dues.

"Hm," Diana said to herself as Morgan approached her.

She turned to her daughter and noticed an unusual glow about her. She was dolled up and had pulled her hair up into a ninja bun. She wore a cute maroon velvet tube top, shorts, and a pair of thigh-high boots that matched her top. She normally was in a chipper mood, but Diana paid close attention to the smile that seemed to be glued to her face.

"We're almost out of Casamigos," Morgan said, looking at the clipboard in her hand. "And the new getups you ordered the girls are downstairs. I told them that they're for the Barbie show you have planned for them, but those hoes are trying to wear them tonight. I'ma end up slapp . . . What?" Morgan stopped talking when she saw the creepy smirk Diana was giving her.

"Who is he?"

"Whaaat?" Morgan asked, and her face instantly flushed. That gave Diana all the confirmation she needed. "I don't know what you're talking about."

"I'll let you tell me on your own. But let me tell you something, that little stupid smile you have on your face? I wore it all the time when it came to your father," Diana said and gave a happy giggle at the memories. "But I already put in an order for the Casamigos. It will be here tomorrow. And as far as those outfits, put them in your office, because those girls will sneak into them tryin'a be cute."

"Got it."

"And, Morgan? When you're done with that, bring Waterfall to me."

"Got it."

Seeing that everything was under control, Diana slipped away to her office. She shut the door and took off her pumps to slide on her Chanel slippers. She then sat at her desk, pulled her money counter close, and grabbed a thick stack of hundreds. A few of the girls owed on their dues, and she hoped they were out there working, handling their business. Diana hated when the count was off.

She was learning that some took her recent health battles and distractions for leniency. She didn't like it one bit. Morgan had done a good job holding down the fort, but if she was going to take over completely, she was going to have to learn to bring the hammer down. There was a knock on her door, and Diana set down the stack of hundreds in her hand.

"Come in."

Morgan opened the door and walked through, but she wasn't alone. With her was Waterfall. It was her tall and thick figure that Diana knew would make her a moneymaker. The men went crazy for her hazel eyes and almond-colored skin, but she was among the women who were late on their dues. Even on a slow night she was taking home at least a thousand dollars, which was why her owing didn't make any sense.

"Sit." Diana pointed at the empty seat across from her desk.

Waterfall sat down with a blatant attitude and looked at her fingernails. Diana was deciding whether to be offended or intrigued by the nerve of her. The bikini getup she wore wasn't one of the ones Diana provided. In fact, it looked custom-made, and Diana could tell by the clarity that the diamonds embroidered at the neck were real. She stared at Waterfall until the girl reluctantly looked back at her.

"Yes?" Waterfall asked like Diana was bothering her.

"Is there a problem?"

"There's money out there, Diana. I don't know why she brought me back here to you."

"You've been with me for years, Waterfall. Or should I say Angelica?" Diana started speaking smoothly. "You know what I like and what I don't like. There's no point of you being in my club making money if you aren't bringing it to me. You are two weeks behind on your dues, and you know I don't play about my money."

"Yeah, so?"

"Yeah, so?" Diana repeated and scoffed.

"I'll pay my dues tonight when I get the money, a'ight? Why you sweatin' me about some little change?"

"Because it was supposed to be paid already."

"How would you know what I paid and haven't paid? It ain't like you've been here to notice."

"Waterfall, you ain't paid shit," Morgan told her, and Waterfall smacked her lips.

"I remember you used to be cool, Morgan. Now you're all up her ass snitchin' and shit."

"I don't have to say shit. The books don't lie. You haven't signed off on your dues in two weeks, which means you haven't paid."

"Whatever."

She flared her nose and rolled her eyes. She was too comfortable acting that way, which let Diana know she'd been acting that way for a while.

"This is how she talks to you?" she asked her daughter.

"Sometimes." Morgan shrugged.

"Well, it will never happen again. Come slap the fuck out of her."

Waterfall smirked like she knew Morgan wasn't going to do a thing. Morgan saw it too. Waterfall even went so far as to look Morgan up and down and then look at Diana.

"This bitch ain't gon' do shit to me," she said with a laugh. "And I heard you were too busy getting shot up in the streets. You probably would go into cardiac arrest tryin'a handle me."

Diana almost stood up to get to her, but Morgan beat her to it. She backhanded Waterfall so hard she fell out of the chair. But she didn't stop there. She kicked her hard in the gut, too. Waterfall tried to curl up in a fetal position, but Morgan snatched her up by her hair and forced her back in her seat.

"Watch your fucking mouth when you speak to her," Morgan told her. "And from now on, watch how you speak to me too. Got it?"

Waterfall nodded her head, and that prompted Morgan to backhand her again. And again and again.

"I didn't hear you," Morgan huffed. "Do you got it?"

"Yes, ma'am."

"Y'all have been taking my niceness for weakness around this motherfucka, and that stops now."

"Yes, ma'am." Morgan might have been done with her, but Diana wasn't. Waterfall looked at her with tears in her eyes. "Diana, I am—"

"An idiot," Diana finished for her. "The nerve of you to come in front of me, wearing diamonds that you paid for with the money you owe me. I made you, which means I could destroy you. Should I kill her, Morgan?"

"I mean, she isn't paying you anyway. She's just taking up space. So many girls would kill to work here."

"I won't mess up again!" Waterfall cried. "I'll give you your money! All of it! You can have it all."

"Your change in tune is funny," Diana told her and pulled a Ruger from her desk. "You're lucky I want my money. Go get it, plus everything you've made tonight. Or I'm going to fill your body up with every bullet in this magazine. You have five minutes."

"Yes, ma'am!"

Waterfall scrambled out of the room. When she was gone, Morgan watched Diana put the gun away.

"I thought you were going to kill her," she said.

"I wanted to. Badly. Business isn't usually nice. I made an exception today." Diana picked up her landline and dialed security downstairs. When they answered, she said, "Make sure Waterfall doesn't leave the building until she brings me my money."

When Diana hung up, she went back to counting, and Morgan sat down on one of her couches. Three Dominican men came in not too long after Diana made the phone call, with Waterfall in tow. In her hands was a big bag of money. She set in on the floor next to Diana's desk and looked regretfully at it.

"It's all there," she said sadly.

"You're on bartending for the rest of the week," Diana told her and waved them out of the office.

When they left, Diana could feel Morgan's eyes burning a hole in her forehead. She tried to ignore it but couldn't. It was like a puppy begging for a bite of food. She sighed and stopped counting again.

"Do you want to say something?"

"No," Morgan answered.

"Mm-hmm. Well, since you're going to be staring at me like a stalker, how about you tell me how things are going with Boogie and the rest?"

"We finally met with Ming," Morgan answered, and Diana raised her brows.

"Really? How'd you pull that off?"

"It was all Boogie's doing. He has some inside person on the Chinese side."

"Interesting."

"Whoever it is gave him the scoop on where Ming would be, and we snatched him up."

"I'm sure he wasn't too happy about that."

"Nope. But we were able to come to a resolve. A peaceful one."

"So the Chinese are back in the fold?" Diana asked hopefully.

"Not exactly. Ming agreed to the truce, but he doesn't want to have anything to do with us. We can't do business in the BX, and he has agreed to stay out of our boroughs."

"The question is, can we trust his word?"

"We just have to wait and see, I guess." Morgan shrugged.

"Damn." Diana wasn't able to hide the sadness in her voice.

"What?"

"The five seats have truly turned into four."

"Well, technically with Staten Island, it's still five."

"Nevertheless, things as I knew them have come to an end. It's funny, because I know nothing lasts forever, but

I was hoping for a little more time. But this is just a reminder of how fast things can change, and so drastically, too."

"It might not be all bad. We got a win. A small one, but still a win," Morgan told her, and she smiled.

"Yeah . . . maybe you're right."

Diana called it a night early and left the club in Morgan's hands. She was tired and wanted to rest up before her trip in a few days. She hadn't told Morgan yet, but she was planning to go on vacation. It had been so long since she was able to take one. All she wanted to do was wake up on a mountaintop and just exist in time and space. Now that Morgan was there, she would be able to. Although Diana worried about her, she had proven to be capable of handling all Diana's affairs. Diana guessed they were her affairs now.

The club was set to close in a few hours, but cars were still coming and going. Diana was escorted to the back seat of the vehicle that would get her home, but she stopped before she got in. A BMW was slowing up on her, and she couldn't help but to watch. She placed a hand in her purse and wrapped her fingers around her gun. The first thought she had was that it could be Ming. Maybe he had lied about the truth and still wanted to knock all of the old players off the board. But when the car stopped and rolled the window down, Diana saw that it wasn't Ming after all.

"Diana. Long time no see."

"What are you doing here, Louisa?"

Chapter 22

May 2001

"State your business," a voice blared from the speaker outside of a tall brass gate.

"Eduardo, open this damn gate! Marco knows I'm coming," Diana shouted from the window of her car.

"My apologies, Miss Diana. Please, come through."

There was a soft clank that sounded when the gate opened. She pulled her Bentley through and made her way up the remainder of the drive, making sure to wave at Eduardo. He was sitting in his security post, eating what looked like a sandwich. She parked behind one of Marco's many cars and got out. Her heels clicked and clacked on the concrete as she made her way up the stairs and to the front door. It opened the moment she approached, and she smiled at Marco's help, Antonia.

"Where is he?" she asked, removing her big shades from her face.

"In the study, ma'am. But he is in a meeting right now. Would you like a glass of wine while you wait?"

"A meeting with who?" Diana asked curiously and followed Antonia to the kitchen.

"I do not know. He has been in there for over an hour though."

Diana sat down at the glass table in the kitchen area and let Antonia bring her a glass of wine. She sipped it and checked the time on the oven clock. Marco knew she didn't like to wait. He would surely be hearing her mouth when he was done with whatever meeting he was in.

"Don't you think it's a little early to be drinking?" a voice sounded.

Diana smiled when she recognized the voice of Marco's wife, Christina. She placed the wineglass down and turned to face the beautiful woman. Christina's full head of long hair flowed gracefully around her made-up face. She wore a red dress that hugged every curve and a pair of black heels.

"Well, well, well. Don't you look fancy," Diana commented, looking her up and down.

"Yes, see my husband is supposed to take me to lunch while the kids are at school. But you are butting into those plans."

"Put the claws away. I'm just here to double-check one of my orders. One of my guys made a mistake."

"You couldn't do that over the phone?"

"Now, Christina, you know I'm hands-on. But it looks to me like we're both waiting on that husband of yours. Antonia said he is in another meeting."

Diana watched Christina's face drop into an annoyed expression. It sparked her attention. Who was Marco in a meeting with?

"I don't even know why he would bring that filth into my house."

"Whoa, let's rewind." Diana set her wineglass down on the table. She pulled a chair out and motioned for Christina to sit with her. "Who is Marco in his study with?"

"The devil herself," Christina said when she sat down. "His sister Louisa."

"Wait, sister? I thought his sister lived in Nebraska."

"That's the one I like. This one not so much."

"I didn't know he had another sister."

"Because she is loco, that one. Something isn't right in her head. The kids don't even know about her."

"Why?"

"You didn't just hear me? She's loco. A complete nut job. Louisa is a child from a previous relationship, and when they were younger, she used to cause Marco's mother so much grief. Can you believe that? A woman who took you in."

"What did she used to do?"

"Marco didn't go into too much detail, but he did tell me one time she poured bleach into his mother's soap and shampoo. And he said Louisa used to physically abuse his other siblings. But not him. She took a strange liking to him. So much so that she tried to sabotage our wedding."

"What happened?"

"I was never actually able to prove it was her. But the wedding dress that I really liked was set on fire, my hair and makeup never showed up, and the cake? I don't even want to tell you about the cake. That, among many other things, went terribly wrong. It almost went down as the worst day of my life, but my Marco made it all better. I think he knew. Because when I said she wasn't welcome in my home or in our future children's lives, he didn't object."

"So why is she here now?"

"She showed up unannounced wanting to talk to Marco. Inventory, I guess. Marco must be placing an order."

"Placing an ord . . . wait. Are you telling me that his sister Louisa is his connect?"

"Yes. She found a loophole back into our lives. You might not know, but his old supplier, Diablo, got caught up big time with the Feds. Marco didn't want his hands in any of that. Louisa heard about Diablo's legal issues and offered to connect him to everything he needed. And I have to give it to her—with his business and all of your business, she has built quite the life for herself in Florida. Queenpin status. Marco told me that she would stay in check because she needs all of you. But I still do not like her, and today will be her first and last time in my home."

The two women stopped talking when they heard laughter in the distance. Shortly after, Marco appeared in the kitchen with a woman wearing a skirt suit. Diana didn't need more than one guess to know the woman was Louisa. She was very easy on the eyes and wore a smile from ear to ear. It faded as soon as she saw Christina sitting there. In fact, Diana swore she saw the woman cut her eyes. Christina stood up and walked directly up to the two of them.

"Don't you ever show up unannounced to my home ever again, do you understand?"

"Christina," Marco tried to intervene, but Christina held up a hand.

"No, DeMarco. I only allowed this because it was business and the children weren't home. But what if they were? I do not want them to know this loco woman!"

"Oh, Christina, is this still about the mishaps that happened at your wedding?" Louisa asked innocently. "I thought we were over this. I told Marco next time he has an event to keep a closer eye on things. Maybe I would have stuck around."

"DeMarco might not be able to see you for what you are, but I do. You are evil. Pure evil! I want her out of my house now! I never want her here again!"

"Tsk tsk tsk, a friend of yours?" Louisa had an amused expression and glanced at Diana.

"More like family, but apparently you might not be able to relate," Diana responded tersely.

"Uh-huh." Louisa and Diana had a miniature stare down before a slow smile formed on Louisa's lips. "You're Diana?"

"I guess that depends on who's asking."

"The person who just corrected your order. Tread lightly. I wouldn't want it to get lost in limbo," Louisa told her with a wink.

She placed her sunglasses on her face, kissed Marco on the cheek, and left the home.

That was the first and last time Diana had ever seen Louisa. The last thing she remembered about that day was Christina cursing Marco out in Spanish. Diana never spoke about the incident with Marco. She also never brought up how she knew Louisa was his connect. She didn't feel like it was any of her business. As long as she got the things she needed on time, then all was good. Still, she knew that Louisa showing up after all that time couldn't have been good news.

"I can't come visit the place my brother seemed to love so much?" Louisa asked, batting her long eyelashes.

"I don't see why you would want to do that, being that you didn't even come to his funeral."

"That's because that wretched wife of his never even got word to me that Marco was . . . was . . ." Louisa's voice wavered for a second before she regained control. "That Marco was no longer with us. I wouldn't have missed it for the world."

"Well, how did you find out that he died?"

"I spoke with my nephew," Louisa told her and watched the shock wave cross Diana's face. "And my niece. I saw them, too."

"When? How? I thought Christina kept them from you."

"She should have known eventually they would find out about me. Especially since Lorenzo has taken over for his father. But maybe she is still too sick with grief to have thought that far into it. You would think she would be a little more grateful to me. Especially since it's because of me she has everything she needs."

"I'm sure Marco would have made a way without you."

"Maybe, but he didn't."

"Ha! Do you really think that?" Diana asked, truly tickled. "You can try to act all high and mighty now that he's gone, but you know just like I know that Marco is the reason you are where you are today. Without him and us, your little weapons business would have never taken root to make way for everything else you've become. Humble yourself."

If looks could kill, Diana would have been dead where she stood. For the second time in their lives, the two of them had a stare down. Finally, Louisa chuckled and blew Diana a kiss.

"I'll be seeing you, Diana."

She rolled her window up and drove away. Once again, Diana had a bad feeling about Louisa being in town. Maybe she was there to finally get to know her niece and nephew, but Diana felt like there was more to it. She just didn't know what. A chill came over her. That woman had some bad energy surrounding her.

Chapter 23

Since the meeting with Ming a few days before, Boogie still found himself looking over his shoulder sometimes. It would probably be a hard habit to break. He was sure nobody could link the body that he had dropped in Chinatown back to him, but he wanted to be cautious, just until he was positive that Ming held up his end of the bargain. Still, he couldn't help but to feel optimistic. New days were upon them, and maybe he could finally start his healing process. He had never had time to really mourn his dad. And even though his mom had done an evil thing to him, she had still been his mom. His last punishment to her had been that he hadn't gone to her funeral. But he was done harboring those ill feelings. It was time to put their memories to rest in a healthy way. He just had to figure out how.

He drove alone through the streets of Brooklyn, making his way to Big Wheels, the automotive shop he owned. When he got there, his phone began to vibrate, and when he looked down, he saw that it was Bentley calling.

"Hello?"

"Damn, nigga. I feel like a bitch blowing you up like this. If it weren't for Morgan and Roz, I wouldn't even know you were alive."

"My bad, G. I've just been handling a few things on my own."

"No doubt. I'm not tripping. I'm just surprised you haven't called to see how your numbers are looking. The young'uns been puttin' in work. They're over their dues for the month, too."

"Good shit."

"Yup. And I heard about the shit with the Chinese, too."

"Yeah. About that—put the word out and make sure none of ours make any hits in the Bronx. I don't even want them hired by anybody in Brooklyn. Ever."

"It's already done."

"Good."

"Ay, Boogie? Are you sure you're cool? It's not like you to go all incognito like this."

"Yeah, I'm straight. Like I said, I'm just handlin' a few things. Speakin' of which, I'm about to get off this phone. I'ma holler at you."

"Yup. I just pulled up to check on Roz anyway, so I'll see you when I see you."

When they got off the phone, Boogie asked himself why he didn't tell him about Adam popping up at the hospital. He didn't know if it was pride in the way. Or maybe he just didn't want to hear Bentley say that he should allow Adam to be in Amber's life. Either way, it just wasn't a conversation he wanted to have.

He had eyes on Adam ever since that day though. He knew he got a job as a forklift driver at a local warehouse. He knew he stayed in an apartment in the Bronx, which was good for him given the new agreement. And Boogie also knew that he had gone back up to the hospital. He'd asked Sandra to call him and tell him if Adam came sniffing around again. Sure enough, he did. Boogie couldn't help to think that Adam wanted more to do with Roz than Amber. And Boogie wasn't letting go of either.

"My man Boogie!" a young cat named Don Don said when Boogie rolled his Lamborghini truck up to the garage. Boogie reached out the window and shook his hand. "What can I do you for?"

Don Don recently was released from jail, and Boogie had given him a job when no one else would. He worked in the garage and learned the trade while working. He was serious about his money and always showed up on time to work.

"Just wash her real good for me. I'm gon' be inside for a while."

"I got you!"

Boogie got out of the vehicle so that he could pull it into the garage. When Boogie walked inside Big Wheels, he moved around the automotive customers and went to the back offices. He had to pass Julius's on his way, and he couldn't help but to stop and look inside. It had been completely cleared out, but Boogie still could envision him sitting at his desk. Julius had been Barry's best friend and someone Boogie had considered an uncle. He was one of the people responsible for sending Boogie's life spiraling down with his greed. Him killing Barry had caused the first domino to drop. There were still times Boogie couldn't believe it. Not wanting to let his emotions get the best of him, Boogie reached and shut the door.

When he finally got to his father's office, now his, he sat at the desk and leaned back. His eyes fluttered along the walls at the family pictures hanging up, and he felt a little lighter. That was how he wanted to remember Barry, exactly how he looked in those pictures: happy. His eyes lingered a little longer on the photo of the two of them. Boogie couldn't have been more than 13 years old. Barry had taken him fishing, and Boogie had gotten a big catch. Barry was so proud of him that day. That was a long time ago, though. Emiko had said she was sure Barry would have been proud of him now. If only she knew how badly he wished he could hear those words directly from his father.

Boogie closed his eyes and let his mind wander to all the times he'd been able to tell Barry that he loved him. He didn't say it as often as he could have, but he liked to think he said it enough. It was time to let all the hurt he was harboring go. He sighed and his lips started moving.

"Pop, life ain't been easy since you left. I guess you can say I took you for granted. I'm sure I'm not the only one who thought their old man would live on forever. But here I am, livin' without you. You made me stronger than I ever knew I could be, and that's how I know I'll be okay. Just watch over me, a'ight? I love you, and I know you loved me. Oh, and PS, I'm sorry that Mama was such a bitch. I'll talk to you soon."

When Boogie opened his eyes, he felt tears in the corners of them. He wiped the water away and sniffled. He hadn't said much, but he had said enough. He gave the office one more look around before leaving. Maybe next time he could spend more time there, but there was one other thing he'd come to Big Wheels for.

"I'm almost done with her, Boog!" Don Don told him when he saw Boogie enter the garage. "I just need to wax the tires."

"No rush," Boogie told him. "I actually came out here to holler at you real quick."

"Man, if it's about eating Tommy's sandwich, I already told the nigga sorry. It just looked so delicious just sitting there in the fridge. I had to have it!"

"What? No. I don't give a damn about a sandwich."

"Oh." Don Don paused and glanced wide-eyed at him. "Well, just forget I even said anything."

"You're a fool," Boogie laughed and sat down on an upside-down crate. "But nah, on a serious tip. You did your bid in Bayview, right?"

"Yeah."

"I want to know if you happened to come across somebody while you were on the inside."

"Give me a name, and I'll let you know if I know 'em," Don Don said as he sprayed the last tire.

"Adam McGregory."

"Adam?" He chuckled. "It's funny you bring him up. Yeah, I knew that fool. He was cool. I used to bust his ass on the spades table."

"What can you tell me about him?"

"Besides the fact that he got locked up for stealing a little-ass five bands? I know he had a girl he couldn't wait to get out and see. Said they had a kid."

"Anything else?"

"Nah. He wasn't really a street dude from what I could tell. Just a nigga caught on the wrong end of the law. Why? Is everything good with him?"

"I was just askin' some questions. That's all."

"You sure? 'Cause that's him right there. He made an appointment earlier this morning to get an oil change on his Impala. If shit ain't square . . ."

Boogie stood up and looked outside at an Impala pulling up. Sure enough, it was Adam who stepped out of the car wearing a camouflage hoodie. No wonder Don Don said it was funny he'd brought up Adam's name. Of all the automotive shops in Brooklyn, he chose Big Wheels to get an oil change. Boogie didn't say anything when he walked out of the garage.

"You've got some nerve showin' up here."

"What? A brotha can't get an oil change?" Adam asked innocently.

"Anywhere but here you can."

"Fine, I'll go somewhere else," he said, but he didn't budge.

"Somethin' else I can help you with?"

"You know, after I left the hospital, I did some digging on you. And you have quite the rep, Bryshon Tolliver."

"Do I?"

"You do. Word on the street is you run an underground ring of thieves."

"Good thing I don't listen to the word on the streets," Boogie responded with a straight face.

"Come on, man, put me on to something. I just got out. You already got the girl. I just want to put some money in my pockets."

"Nigga, you sound like a cop. You wearin' a wire?"

"So hostile, but we both know what this is about." Adam smirked smugly. "You can't stand the fact that I used to stick my dick all up in your bitch. I even got that pussy pregnant. Damn, you're really a simp-ass nigga when I think about it."

His mistake was realized when the last word was out of his mouth. He didn't even have time to get on defense. Boogie snatched him up by his hoodie and slammed him on the hood of his Impala. Before he spoke, he checked to make sure Adam really wasn't wearing a wire. He wasn't, but that meant he was taunting Boogie just because he wanted to.

"I don't know what you're playin' at or why you haven't left town yet, but I'ma give you twenty-four hours to make that happen. If you're still here after that, let's just say that you won't be for long."

Boogie tossed him to the ground, and Adam hopped up like he was about to do something. He had a savage look in his eyes, and his hand flew to the back of his waist. But a red dot appearing on his chest stopped him from drawing his weapon. Then another appeared on his stomach, and another on his crotch. He looked down at his body and then glared at Boogie.

"Like I said, make sure you're gone from New York by tomorrow," Boogie said.

Chapter 24

"Amber! Stop it before you fall off this bed. Girl, I said stop!"

Roz's tired voice travelled out into the hallway, and it was followed by Amber's wild giggles. She was giving her mom a run for her money, not knowing or understanding that she didn't have the energy to keep up with her. Boogie had shown up at the right time then. He swooped Amber up into the air when he came into the room and flew her around like an airplane.

"Are you in here givin' your mama a hard time?" he asked and tickled her.

When she had enough, he pretended to slam her into the bed. She loved when he did that and instantly came back for more. Roz relaxed back into her body pillow, looking relieved that he was there. She smiled as she watched the two of them play. Eventually Amber crawled back into her arms, and Boogie went into the bathroom to shower. When he came back out, gone were his street clothes, replaced with a pair of pajama pants and a T-shirt.

"You're in for the night?" Roz asked, feigning shock.

"You surprised?"

"I just don't remember the last time you called it a night at, let's see . . ." She checked the digital clock on the wooden nightstand beside the bed. "Nine o'clock? Wow, I actually think this is a first."

"Now I know you're lyin'," he told her and climbed in the bed with them. "But either way, there's nowhere else I'd rather be right now than with you."

He pulled her close to him and kissed her forehead. She nestled into his body while holding Amber tightly so she wouldn't try to climb out of the bed. Boogie hurried to turn on a family movie that they could watch together.

"How was your day?" Roz asked when Amber's attention was completely on the television.

"Boring. Just moved around a little bit. Nothin' major," Boogie said without looking at her.

He didn't want to look her in the eyes when he knew that he was lying. He'd already done that with the house. But he didn't want to talk about what had happened between him and Adam. If he knew what was good for him, he would heed Boogie's warning and be out of their lives the next day.

"Mm-hmm," Roz commented and stared at him.

"What?"

"You're not telling me something. What is it?"

"Nothin', girl. I just handled some business, that's all. Since when have you been interested in the details of street shit?"

"Ever since I found out that you lied about the reason we're staying in Caesar's place. Why didn't you tell me the truth about the house?"

There it was. Boogie should have known he wouldn't be able to keep the wool over her eyes for long. He finally looked at her and expected to see anger written all over her face, but instead there was concern.

"How did you find out?"

"Being on bed rest, I've had a lot of time to catch up on things I've missed. Like the fire that took place in our neighborhood. The one that burned down our house."

"Roz . . ."

"Talk to me, Boogie. I'm fragile, but I'm not dead. What's been going on?"

"Stuff that I got handled. But about the house, I should have told you. But at the time I couldn't. You had just woken up, and I didn't want to fuck you up with that shit. Especially after the fight we had before . . . you know."

"I do wish you had told me, but that wouldn't bring back all my stuff and pictures."

"Nothin' like that will ever happen again, I promise."

"Don't. Please don't make promises you don't know if you can keep," she said, and when he tried to speak again, she placed a finger to his lips. "I love you so deeply, Bryshon Tolliver. I'ma ride regardless."

"You shouldn't have to."

"If I were with somebody else, I wouldn't have to. But my heart chose you. I almost died, and when I woke up, all I thought about was my family. And you are my family. I know now that there is no other place I'd rather be than with you."

She kissed him softly on the lips, and he returned it. He didn't know what he had done to deserve something so good. But he wanted to hold on to it for as long as he had breath in his body. Amber climbed over Roz and squeezed between the two of them. She looked up at Boogie and flashed her tiny teeth.

"Dadadadada," she said over and over, melting his heart.

"You are her dad. You know that, right?" Roz said and sighed. "I know we haven't talked about Adam, but I don't . . . I don't want to. When I woke up and saw him sitting there, I . . . I was so scared. Boogie, I was so scared. But then I saw you, and I cried tears of joy because I knew you wouldn't let him hurt me."

"Hurt you? What you mean, hurt you?"

"Adam was abusive, Boogie. He used to hit me, and when he found out I was pregnant, he . . ." Roz stopped, and her lip quivered. "He, um, he tried to kill her. He beat me so bad that day."

"Why didn't you tell Bentley? I know he wouldn't have gone for that."

"I didn't have to. He went to jail the next day for robbing that bank. They gave him five years. I didn't think he would get out so soon. But, Boogie, I don't want him anywhere near us."

"You won't have to worry about that," Boogie told her and placed his forehead on hers. "That I can promise you. I'll body that nigga before he ever lays a hand on you again."

"Okay," Roz exhaled gratefully.

He held the two of them until he heard their breathing get shallow. They were asleep before the movie even ended. His stomach growled loudly, reminding him he hadn't eaten anything for dinner. Carefully, so he wouldn't wake them up, he climbed out of bed and left the room. Although Boogie had been to Caesar's home plenty of times, it still was easy to almost get lost. He managed to find his way to the kitchen, got a plate from a cabinet, then went to the fridge to make a sandwich.

"You can go ahead and make two of those. It looks like we were thinking the same thing."

Boogie stopped putting mayonnaise on his bread and looked at the newcomer. Milli, Caesar's daughter, had come in and sat at the table. She too was wearing pajamas. The only difference was the bonnet on top of her head.

"No problem," Boogie said and grabbed another plate.

When he finished, he took the two sandwiches to the table and sat down. She thanked him and took one of the plates, not hesitating to dig in. The two of them filled their stomachs in silence until the food was gone.

"I haven't seen you around here much lately," he said after swallowing his last bite.

"That's because you haven't been here much."

"Touché. What's new?"

"Just getting ready to be without my daddy again," she said, and Boogie sat up straighter.

"Somethin' wrong with Caesar?"

"He's actually better than I've seen him in a while. So much so that he's going on vacation. He and Diana are going to the Virgin Islands. You know, I don't remember the last time he took a break from work. But since Nicky's been running the show, I guess now is as good a time as ever."

"You know, I almost didn't take him seriously when he said he was steppin' down. Because who would want to give up all of this? The money, the power, and the respect." Boogie smiled in spite of himself. "But when I thought about it, I realized there's still a lot more to life than just that shit. Caesar, Diana, and my pops spent all of their lives buildin'. It's time to start enjoyin', and I wish my pops were alive to enjoy that part of the journey."

"You'll just have to enjoy it for him," Milli said.

"Nah, I got a lot of buildin' to do. I'm new blood runnin' an old empire. I'm still findin' my way."

"That's the cool part about being the new blood then, isn't it? You get to make your own recipe. Get the money, power, and respect, but don't forget to enjoy life in the process. Figure out who you are outside of what you do." She reached across the table and squeezed his hand in a comforting manner before standing up. "But I'm about to call it a night. I have an exam coming up, and I need as much rest as I can get."

"Good night," Boogie said.

She left, but her words stayed with him. Who was he outside of what he did? He'd dived so deeply into the game he didn't even know what it was like to resurface from it. At one point, he had dreams of cooking in his own restaurant. Did he even like to cook anymore? He'd been close to getting his degree when his father died. Would he want to go back to school to finish? He hadn't had the time to think about those things. But since the feud was over, maybe he could find some.

Chapter 25

"Agh!"

The shout was followed by a thud as Adam's fist put a hole in the wall. He was standing in the entryway of his apartment reeling with anger. He couldn't believe Boogie had put his hands on him like that. He'd even driven around for hours to blow off steam, but it didn't work, because there he was destroying property. Adam wished the wall was Boogie's face. How had Roz, his Roz, gotten mixed up with him? He was so overwhelmed with emotions that he just threw his hands over his head before he put more holes in the wall.

When he was released from incarceration, Adam thought that his life was taking a turn for the better. He thanked God that he didn't use a gun when he robbed the bank because he would have been still rotting in a jail cell for armed robbery. He had high hopes of getting his family back and making up for all of his past mistakes. Even though Roz had never returned any of his letters and had even changed her number on him, it was all he fantasized about. No matter how long he was away from her, she was his. It was fate when he got the hospital call about her. He thought back to the first time he saw her in such a long time.

He stood in the door of the hospital for what felt like hours. Really it was only a few minutes. He watched as the nurse tried to feed Roz, but eventually she just took the spoon in her weak hand and fed herself. Adam found himself smiling. She hadn't changed, still as stubborn as he remembered. When the nurse left, she smiled as she bustled by him. Roz still hadn't seen him. He had so many emotions rushing through him, and he didn't know which one to show: happiness, sadness . . . or anger. That was the one he was trying his hardest to keep at bay. Maybe she had a good reason to stay away. Maybe . . .

"Roz?" he finally said.

She looked up quickly, happily when she heard his voice, but the moment she saw that it was him, the smile faded. She had been expecting someone else. That much was obvious. But who? He stepped inside the room and just took in her beautiful face. She hadn't changed at all. She was still the prettiest girl he had ever laid eyes on.

"Adam? What are you doing here?"

Those were her first words to him. "What are you doing here?" He almost couldn't believe his ears. Or his eyes. She wasn't happy to see him. It was all in her body language.

"The hospital called me," he said and took the liberty of sitting down next to her bed. "I was listed as your emergency contact."

"Well, that was a mistake. How are you—"

"Free? I was released a few weeks ago. You would know that if you read any of my letters. Did you?"

"No." She shook her head.

"Did you get them?" he asked, cutting his eyes at her.

"Yes," she breathed and glanced at the door.

"The nurse left. It's just me and you. And I want you to tell me why you left me to rot in that prison by myself."

"Adam, please."

"I thought about you every day, you know that? And you couldn't read a letter or send me a single photo of my fucking daughter!"

She jumped at the rising of his voice. He watched her bottom lip tremble, but he didn't care about her sadness. Suddenly her beauty didn't matter, and he felt the anger taking over. He remembered how mad she used to make him all the time and how he used to have to punish her for it.

"You're still a bad girl, I see. Even after all this time. You probably thought you would never see me again. Didn't you?"

"Adam, I—"

"Didn't you?"

She jumped again and tried to reach for the remote to page the nurse. She wasn't fast enough. Adam moved it far out of her reach.

"Where is my daughter, Roz?"

"She's with Bentley."

"I never liked your brother," Adam said. "Where is he so I can get her?"

"I won't tell you. She doesn't even know you."

"Whose fault is that?"

"Yours!" she said with a fire in her eyes, one he never saw before.

"Well, it looks like you finally grew a backbone. I didn't come here for this, but I guess since I'm back, I should remind you what I do to bad girls."

He leaned forward so that he could reach for her hand. But right as he was stretching his arm, someone entered the hospital room. It was a tall man who Adam had never seen before. Adam instantly dropped his arm and sat up straight. He watched how Roz instantly teared up when she saw him. And by the way the man looked at her, Adam could tell he loved her. He knew then where the fire in Roz's eyes had come from. It was him. He was her savior.

"I shoulda just killed him then," Adam said to himself, snapping back into reality. "I shouldn't have let him leave that hospital alive."

Roz had done more than just move on. She was with a king of New York. Adam had let his emotions lead him to the autobody shop even after learning who Boogie really was. For some reason, he still wanted to test the waters. It wasn't until Boogie snatched him out that he realized the waves might have been a little too high for him. But Boogie's flex of power didn't do anything but make Adam even more livid. Boogie had demanded that he be gone within twenty-four hours, and Adam didn't know how he was going to make that happen. But it was shown that he could be removed from the chessboard with a snap of his fingers.

"I wanna kill that nigga." He was still murmuring under his breath when he walked into his kitchen.

"I can make that happen."

The voice made Adam jump like there were ants in his pants. He didn't have a gun, so he snatched a knife from its holder and waved it in the direction of where he'd heard the voice. The living room lamp turned on, and the person who flipped the switch smiled at him from his couch.

"Adam, my name is Louisa. And I think we can help each other out."

Chapter 26

Louisa watched Adam swing the knife like a madman. She wanted to laugh because it was no match for the SIG nestled in her Celine clutch. She sat comfortably on his hard, cheap couch and waited for him to get done trying to scare her.

"Bitch! What you still just sitting there for? Get the fuck out of my house!"

"I would barely call this a house," she chuckled and looked around at his box of an apartment. "A closet maybe. Actually, my closet is bigger than this."

"Well, if you're so rich, why don't you go back to where you came from? Why are you in my spot talking shit?"

"Didn't you just hear me say that I think we can help each other out?"

"The only thing you might be able to help me with is some pussy. Other than that, I'm good."

"Watch the things you say to me, because what I'll do to you is much worse than just hemming you up and telling you to leave town." Her words were icy and caught him right in the chest.

She smiled as the meaning of her words resonated with him. His mouth opened, and the hand holding the knife fell. She knew. In fact, she had seen and heard the entire ordeal between him and Boogie. She'd been watching from her car.

"What, you been following me or something?"

"Not you."

"That nigga Boogie."

"Yes."

"Well, he's not here."

"I know where I'm at. It wasn't hard to find. Just like it wasn't hard to find out who you are, Adam McGregory. See, money talks wherever I go."

"You did all that footwork just to figure out who I am? There must be a reason for it. What do you want?" Adam asked.

"The same thing you want. To see Boogie knocked off the board. He is the one who swooped in and stole your family from you while you were in jail, isn't he?" Louisa watched his jaw clench and a darkness come over his eyes.

"Even if I do want him dead, it can't happen. He's protected. You do know who he is, right? He runs Brooklyn."

"I'm aware of who he is."

"Then you should know he's damn near untouchable. You saw what happened to me. I don't know what the fuck I was thinking."

"'Damn near' isn't untouchable. It just means we need a plan."

"Wait, who the fuck are you?"

"Do you know who DeMarco Alverez was?"

"Yeah. I remember hearing his name when I was a young'un coming up. He ran Queens. He was a bad motherfucka before he got himself killed."

"He was my brother. And Boogie Tolliver is the reason he's dead."

"So why don't you just kill him yourself?"

"It's complicated, but I can't afford to get my hands dirty . . . yet. I need someone on the inside of the operation who can get close to him. You."

"I'm just going to humor you, lady. What is it that you would want me to do?"

"Become my nephew's new weapons distro. I will provide you with anything he needs, and you will be compensated well for it. I was his connect but—"

"But what? None of this is making sense."

"Ever since his father died, he has been pulling away from me. I don't want to see my brother's empire completely tarnished because my nephew is incompetent," Louisa lied with a straight face.

"Fine," Adam said after a few moments. "But we have a problem. Boogie wants me gone, and I'm sure if you could figure out where I live, he can too."

"Don't worry about that. I have it all covered. I will be in contact with more information. In the meantime, this is your first payment."

Louisa grabbed a bag she'd stashed behind the couch and tossed it to him. When it hit the ground by his feet, a few stacks of money fell out. His eyes opened wide and were glued to it for so long that he didn't even see Louisa get up and walk to the door.

"Like I said, I'll be in touch."

Chapter 27

There was one thing that Zo hated more than anything in the world, and that was lying to his mother. Christina had done a good job raising her kids, and the one thing she'd done the best with was making sure they couldn't lie to her face. Each of her children had a tell if they tried, and she never would let them know what it was. And because of that, Zo had been doing his best to avoid her. Just until things with Louisa were squared away. He also wasn't ready to tell her about Marco's secret life. He didn't know if he ever would be able to. He'd been staying at his condo in Queens and barely answering the phone when she called. However, he found himself craving some of Christina's homemade salsa so much that he somehow found himself at the Alverez family home.

He snuck in the through one of the back doors and checked his surroundings before moving on to the kitchen. He ducked and dodged all of the help. He feared that if they saw him, they would alert his mother. He wanted to be in and out. He finally made it to his destination unseen and let out a breath.

"Salsa, here I come," he said and even did a little dance.

His father always swore that if there were a contest for salsa, Christina would win the first-place award every time. Zo had to agree. It was so good that it had him sneaking into his own home. He opened the fridge door and saw that a fresh jar had recently been made. He grabbed it and was going to get a bowl from a cabinet when he heard footsteps enter the kitchen. He whipped around and saw his mother walking in, holding a plate in her hands. Upon seeing him, she jumped.

"Lorenzo! What the hell? You scared me!"

"I'm sorry, Mama. I was just getting some salsa," he said and held up the jar.

"Well, make a bowl and come sit with me. I haven't seen you. If I had known all I needed to do was make some of that salsa for you to come by here, I would have made a jar every day!"

"Mama, I'm kind of in a rush."

"Too much of a rush for your own mother?" she asked and sat down at the dining room table.

"Never," he said with a sigh.

He was already caught. His mission to get in and out had failed. He made himself a bowl of salsa and grabbed a bag of tortilla chips before sitting across from her. He felt her eyes on him as he began to munch away.

"Where have you been, Lorenzo? I miss having you around."

"I've been around, just handling business. You know."

"Just handling business, eh?"

"Yeah. That's all." Zo looked up at her and smiled. "I'll try to come home more."

"Mm-hmm," Christina said and glanced around the kitchen. She gave a sudden shudder. "It's hard being in here after what happened to Maria and Thomas. I wanted that oven so badly at one point. Now I don't even want to go near it. All I see is Maria . . ."

Her voice trailed off, and she touched her chest with one of her hands. She had to close her eyes for a second and catch her breath. Being Marco's wife for years, seeing dark things was inevitable. Still, Zo knew it hurt her to see her loved ones killed in such a brutal way.

"It's okay, Mama. I'll get you a new stove. I'll redo the whole kitchen if it will make you happy."

"Thank you. But you know what would make me happy?"

"What?"

"If you told me why you were recently in Florida."

Her words caught Lorenzo completely off guard, and he immediately dropped his eyes. How did she know about Florida? He stared at the salsa in his bowl as if he would find an answer there.

"Business," he told her.

"Look at me," she instructed, and instinctively he did what he was told. "What kind of business?"

"Just business, Mama. How do you even know I was there?"

"Daniella told me."

"What else did she say?"

"The same thing as you. That you were there handling business. But I don't know what kind of business could be in Florida. Did you . . . meet anybody there?"

"Mama, just ask what you want to ask," Zo said, knowing when she was beating around the bush. "Just ask me if we met Louisa."

At the mention of her name, a coldness entered Christina's eyes. It was a look Zo had never seen before.

"You met Louisa?"

"Yes, we did."

"I knew it. I knew she would come digging her nose around once she found out DeMarco was dead!"

"Why didn't you or Papa ever tell us about her?"

"We kept her away because there are some things so terrible that no one will believe unless they see them. And the evilness in that woman is one of them. Lorenzo, you must stay away from her! Both you and Daniella. Promise me."

"Why don't you like her? There has to be a reason."

"Do you remember the story of my wedding dress?

"You and Papa used to tell Daniella and me that story all the time. About how somehow it was too close to a candle and went up in flames."

"There's a part in the story that not even your father knew about. Listen closely."

"Christina! You look so beautiful!"

The voice belonged to Christina's longtime friend Kiana. She and the other bridesmaids were marveling over Christina's makeup and hair. While they had smiles on their faces, Christina was a nervous wreck. She sat facing a mirror in her robe that said "Bride" on the back. She gently touched the bun on top of her head and then let her hand fall to her cheek.

"I can't believe I'm getting married."

"I can," Kiana said. "Have you seen the way Marco looks at you? If that isn't love, I don't know what love is."

Christina nodded her head. Kiana was right. Marco loved her and she knew it. Nobody had ever made her feel the way that he did, not even close. That was why she was so nervous. She didn't want to do anything to mess it up.

"Where is the other bridesmaid? Marco's sister," Christina heard someone ask.

"Probably somewhere talking to Marco," Kiana answered. "Christina, you really have your hands full with her. She seems a little off. And have you seen the way she looks at Marco? It's like he's God's gift to man. Creepy."

"Well, one, he is God's gift to man. And two, Marco said that they were close before Louisa was sent away for school." Christina shrugged. "They just rekindled their relationship, and I want her to feel like family. That's why I asked her to be in the wedding."

"As long as you're happy. Now come across the hall to the bridesmaids' dressing room and take a shot of tequila!"

"Kianaaaaa."

"I won't take no for an answer. You're getting married today."

Christina laughed and let Kiana drag her to the other dressing room with the others. She took a shot with them and within minutes felt more at ease. They took photos of her before she told them she was leaving to put her dress on. They still needed to get dressed too, but Kiana said she would be right over to help after. Christina closed the door behind her and stared across the hall. Her dressing room door was wide open. A candle inside was lit, and she could see a shadow flickering along one of the walls. Not only that, but she heard a voice coming from inside. It was whispering something over and over.

Christina stepped forward cautiously until she was in the doorway. At first, she thought it was Marco's mother, but it wasn't. It was Louisa, Marco's sister. She was a gorgeous woman, and she was already wearing her emerald green bridesmaid dress. Christina opened her mouth to speak but stopped once she made out what Louisa was whispering.

"Marco is mine. Nobody will take him from me again. Marco is mine. Nobody will take him from me again."

She kept repeating it while she held something in her hands. It was Christina's wedding dress. She was swaying back and forth slightly and just looking at it while she whispered. Christina took notice of a big bucket of water by her feet. It wasn't there before, so Louisa must have brought it with her. She thought Marco's sister was about to dunk her dress in the water, and she wanted to tell her to stop. But she was frozen. Something had come over her to the point where she couldn't make a peep. Slowly, Louisa looked up from the dress to the flame in the candle. Christina knew what was about to happen next. She wasn't about to dunk the dress, not yet anyway.

"No!" Christina finally found her voice, but it was too late.

Louisa put one of the corners of the dress in the fire, and that was all she wrote. The whole thing went up in flames. Before the fire could touch her fingers, she dropped it in the bucket of water and turned to face Christina.

"Accidents happen," she said with a straight face.

"That . . . that wasn't an accident. You destroyed my dream wedding dress on purpose."

"You mistake my words. The dress isn't the accident I'm speaking of. You are."

"What?"

"I thought he would come to his senses by now and realize just how bad you are for him. But he hasn't, and I can't let him leave me again. Not for you."

"Louisa, what are you talking about? You sound crazy!"

"Don't! Don't ever call me crazy! I'm not crazy, and Marco understands that. He understands me. He's the only thing I have in this world, don't you see? And you're trying to take that from me."

"Louisa, I'm not trying to take him from you. I asked you to be in my wedding to include you."

"No, you did it out of pity. But the moment you're married, you'll take him from me. Just like his mother did. She sent me away. She took my family from me, and I won't take that chance with you."

From one of the folds of her dress she pulled out a switchblade. It was all so fast that Christina only had time to flinch back when Louisa lunged for her neck. She cried out when the blade cut her collarbone, and Louisa smiled big at the sight of the blood.

"I'm going to get rid of your body and tell him that you ran off on him."

"No, please!"

"There's no other way."

Louisa prepared to go in for the kill, but quick foot-steps coming down the hallway stopped her. She hurried and stashed the knife right as Marco's mother, Gabriela, walked in the room.

"Christina, are you okay? I heard you—"

Gabriela stopped talking when she saw the women standing there. Her eyes fell on Louisa, and she gave her the most distasteful look she could muster. Taking one look at the burnt dress in the water and then at Christina's bleeding neck, she didn't ask any questions. She reached in her purse and pulled out a pistol.

"The moment I found out you were going to be in the wedding, I knew the day would go to shit," she said, pointing the gun at Louisa's face. She addressed her next words to Christina. *"Don't worry about the dress, daughter. I brought another one just in case. I just came from the kitchen. She destroyed the cake, too, but we will figure it out."*

"Daughter?" Louisa asked with wavering eyes. *"You call her daughter?"*

"She is what your crazy ass never was to me! Louisa, something has always been wrong with you. I tried, but you . . . you're the devil! And I won't let you ruin Marco's life because of your obsession with him!"

"He's the only one who loves me," Louisa whispered. *"I lost everything else."*

"Well, now you've lost him too," Christina told her. *"You will never be welcome around us or any children we have. Ever. Leave before I let Mama blow your face off."*

"She did say *Abuela* never liked her," Zo said when Christina was done telling the story. "Louisa said that when she was a girl, *Abuela* hated her. That she sent her away for school, and it was years until she saw Papa again."

"That's true. Your *abuela* and *abuelo* did send her away. She had gotten to be too much of a risk in their home."

"What about the wedding? Did she leave?" Zo asked.

"She did. Your *abuela* wasn't playing with that pistol. She wanted a reason to kill that bitch. Your papa was very sad that she wasn't in the wedding though. I never told him what happened because I knew it would break his heart."

"What I don't understand is how they ended up doing business together."

"She made herself an asset," she sighed. "I should have told you right after the funeral. I don't want you doing business with her, Zo. She was supposed to be out of our lives for good."

There was a pleading in her eyes. She was serious, and Zo nodded his head. If he had known that Louisa had tried to kill his mother, he would have told her no in Florida.

"You should have told Papa," Zo told her.

"It's something I regret every day, not telling him back then." She closed her eyes and shook her head. "But your father's businesses were booming. Like I said, she proved herself to be an asset. I didn't want to see the kingdom your father built crumble. But I told him about it right before he died. When I found out about all those trips to Florida."

"You know about the trips to Florida?"

"*You* know about DeMarco's trips to Florida?" Christina asked with a raised brow. "And you didn't say anything?"

"I was trying to figure out what it all meant. I found a bank statement and a number. They led me to Louisa."

"Lorenzo! I wish you had told me before you went to see that *bruja*. What did she tell you?"

"That Papa was planning to leave New York behind. That he was going to start fresh there. Build a new empire. She said she threatened to stop supplying him with inventory and he agreed to come. She told me that he wanted something different for me."

"She's lying!" Christina exclaimed and went into a fit of Spanish curses.

"I wish she were, Mama. I really wish she were, but I saw all the proof with my own two eyes. The bank accounts, the businesses, his house. Mama, he had a house in Florida. He left everything to me."

"Of course he did. He always put your name on any paperwork he filled out. But none of this is as it seems. Louisa is crazy. Oh, my God."

Christina got up and began pacing the kitchen, still saying her curses. Zo knew that when she got like that, the best thing to do was to just leave her alone. She ran her fingers through her hair and took deep breaths to calm down. A few tears even fell from her eyes, but she wiped them away. When she felt stable enough, she turned back to her son.

"She's lying, Lorenzo," she said, jerking her hands. "I found those bank statements too. I was so angry with your father because I didn't know where the money came from and why it was in a Florida bank. So I confronted him. He said that he didn't want to tell me what was going on because he knew how I felt about Louisa. But he told me everything."

"About him wanting to move to Florida?"

"No. There was no force in this world that could make your father leave New York. The businesses are not your father's. She wanted to sign them over to him, but he declined. Did you see any paperwork stating that he owned any of them?"

"No."

"Exactly. The house? She bought it for his birthday last year, so he had someplace to stay when he came to visit. The accounts? They were her accounts. He was secondary at first, but then she made him the primary."

"My name is on those accounts now too."

"Your father was a very smart man. He knew he was mortal. As I said before, anything having to do with money, he put your name on. You were his heir. He trusted you to take care of Daniella and me. Lorenzo, Louisa is delusional. She built a whole life for Marco, and when she told him no, she threatened him. So he told her to do what she feels she has to do. But he was never going to leave Queens. What he built here was meant to last. Before he died, he was supposed to find a new connect. I thought he did. I thought she was out of our lives."

"Why was she so obsessed with Papa?"

"Her mind works different from most people's. She felt that DeMarco was the only person who loved her, and he did. Dearly. She was his blood. But after he saw that she was trying to take over his life, he saw her for what she truly is. There is one last thing you must know, Lorenzo."

"What, Mama?"

"When Louisa was around maybe fifteen or sixteen, and your papa was a little younger than that, Louisa put poison in their food."

"Hers and Papa's?" Zo asked, horrified.

"Yes. She tried to kill him and commit suicide. She wanted the die with the only person she felt loved her. *Abuela* and *Abuelo* didn't send her away to school. They sent her to a psych ward."

Chapter 28

Boogie awoke to the feeling of kisses being planted on his torso. He rubbed his eyes and lifted the comforter only to be met by a grinning Roz. She had a devilish look on her face, and he knew what that meant. She tried to peel his briefs down, but he stopped her by grabbing her hands.

"Roz, we can't. I don't want to hurt you," he told her, and she pouted.

"It's been weeks since I had some dick. I'm horny as fuck, Boogie. My pussy damn near has carpet burns from rubbing orgasms out!"

"Roz," Boogie laughed. He pulled her up to him, trying to get a grip and grow serious again. "Baby, this dick isn't going anywhere. I'm in the horny boat with you, but nothin' matters more to me than you healin' all the way. You got shot and had to get a blood transfusion. That's not some little shit. That's big."

"Boogie, I feel fine! I know you see me running around after Amber now."

"I also see how tired you look right after," Boogie told her and kissed her lips. "I can't fuck you, Roz. Not how I want to."

Roz rolled her eyes at him and reached for her purse on the nightstand. He thought maybe she was going for a vibrator, but that wasn't what she pulled out. She held up a few bills and waved them at him.

"Then what can you do?" she asked. "I got forty dollars."

"So I'm a cheap ho to you?" he asked, laughing hard from his belly.

"You're not cheap and you're not a ho, but this pussy is thumping harder than a club speaker on a Saturday night."

"It's thumpin'?"

"Yes."

"For me?"

"Yes!"

He placed her gently on her back, spread her legs, and got between them. Not being able to make love to her had been difficult. His manhood cried out for her every single day, but he couldn't. Not yet. She was still regaining all of her energy, and he didn't want to do anything that set her back. But he could please her in other ways. He kissed her on the lips tenderly, sucking her tongue and letting her moan into his mouth. Her nipples were erect through her nightgown, and she squirmed underneath him when he pinched them.

"Hsss!" she hissed and followed it with a moan.

He lifted the nightgown over her head and admired her naked body. Every time he saw it, it felt like the first time. His eyes stopped on her stitches, and he felt his face drop.

"Just a battle scar. That's all," she said and kissed him. "I love you, Boogie. But if you make me wait any longer to feel your tongue on my pussy, I'ma kick your ass."

The smile returned to his face, and he scooted down so he could give her what she needed. She was due for a wax, but a little hair never stopped the show. She was a grown woman, and he never minded the stubble. He loved the way she tasted first thing in the morning. Boogie spread her legs wider and parted her fat kitty with his tongue. Once he felt her clit, he sucked it in a pulsating rhythm. She got wetter and wetter, and it turned him on to no end. Gripping her thighs, he rolled over so that she was now on top of his face. He wiped down on her pussy and got as much of her juices as he could and used those to masturbate himself as he continued to give her head.

"Yes! Eat this pussy, Boogie."

Her thighs moved in a circular motion as she made love to his face, and he loved it. He stroked his rock-hard manhood and felt cum coming out of the tip already. With his free hand, he rubbed all over her voluptuous bottom and envisioned himself ramming deep inside of her love canal. He thought about how her walls liked to massage his shaft and how it felt when he came deep inside of her.

"Ahhh!" he moaned breathlessly into her pussy as his body jerked.

He tried to hold his orgasm back for a few more seconds while he sucked her clit more vigorously to force hers out.

"Boogie. Boogie. Boogie!" she moaned, gripping the back of the headboard. "I'm cumming! I'm about to cum on your face, baby. Move."

"Uhn uhn," he said just as she rained down on him.

He jerked again as his nut came shooting out onto the comforter like a volcano. He stroked his tip until the last of it was out, moaning loudly the entire time.

"This was the perfect morning," Roz sighed and fell over onto the bed. While he caught his breath, she grabbed his phone and handed it to him. "Here."

"Why you givin' me this?"

"Bentley called you when you were sleeping. He said something about meeting him in an hour and a half. He said you'll know where."

"And you're just now tellin' me?" Boogie looked at her incredulously.

"Like I said, I was horny. And I wasn't letting you leave this house again without making this kitty purr." She rolled her neck at him playfully and got out of bed to shower. "You got about an hour to make it on time."

"I feel used."

"Don't forget your forty dollars." She winked at him and disappeared into the bathroom.

Boogie pulled the Lamborghini into a place he hadn't been in a long time—Brooklyn. He hadn't been there since his friend and Bentley's cousin, Gino, had been killed. It was his old spot, the place Boogie had first met him. He smiled to himself remembering how he and Bentley had busted up the spot. It had been the start of a beautiful but short-lived friendship. He parked beside Bentley's G-Wagen and got out. Standing guard in front of the apartment complex entrance were two men. They parted when he approached and let him pass. The inside of the apartment smelled like dog piss and looked worse than dog shit. He made his way to the floor Gino's old apartment was on. It wasn't where he lived, but it was where he conducted all of his business.

When Boogie was feuding with the other families, he was inevitably cut off from Marco's gun market. Gino became his guy. He was able to get Boogie any- and everything that he needed, but when Ming killed him, someone else had taken over for him. That someone else was Tweety, Bentley's other cousin. Bentley said he had gotten the name when they were younger because he was skinny like a bird and ate like one. He wasn't so skinny anymore. Tweety was swole and could probably knock a man out with one punch.

When Boogie knocked on the door, it opened within seconds, and a tall, rugged man wearing an eyepatch and a scowl let him step into the living room area of the house. The men standing around were dressed casually, which was a different sight. When Gino was alive, he liked for his people to wear nothing but business attire even if they weren't doing anything but sitting around.

"Damn, Lou, what the fuck happened to you?" Boogie asked.

"That nigga was gettin' some pussy from the wrong bitch!" Bentley said, coming from the back room.

Boogie laughed and the two of them slapped hands.

"Ay, fuck you, Bentley! I ain't know the ho had a nigga, let alone lived with him! Bitch-ass motherfucka stabbed me."

"Damn, Lou. You let a nigga catch you slippin' about some pussy?" Boogie asked, still laughing. "I bet you won't do that no more."

Everybody in the room was cracking up at Lou's expense except him. He didn't find anything funny. He flipped them all off and went back to guarding the door.

"Come on, man," Bentley said, still laughing, and he motioned for Boogie to follow him to the back.

They went back to what would have been the master bedroom but was set up like an office. Tweety was sitting behind the desk counting a stack of money. When he saw Boogie, he stood up and smiled so big the gums over his golds showed.

"Well, if it ain't the boss man himself. How did you like your new shipment?"

"The Glocks were nice. I need to order some more with the sights."

"Yeah," Bentley agreed. "Some of these new niggas can't shoot worth shit, and I don't have time for them fuckin' up on our hits. 'Cause then I gotta deal with the clean-up."

"*You* gotta deal with the clean-up?" Tweety asked and raised a brow.

"I've been busy with other things," Boogie said. "Bentley been holding the streets down for me in the meantime."

"Do the other things you've been busy with have somethin' to do with why you wanted to meet with me today?"

"Somethin' like it," Boogie told him.

"Interestin'." Tweety sat down and gestured for them to sit on a couch he had along the wall.

"I think it smells like expansion outside, don't you?" Boogie asked once he was settled comfortably.

"Does it? I like expansion."

"You should. Lorenzo, Marco's son, is lookin' for a new distro."

"And why is that?"

"Marco's gone, and sometimes what isn't broken still doesn't work for you. And that's the case with Lorenzo," Boogie lied through his teeth. "The old distro isn't his speed. He knew about Gino and all that he did for me."

"What about you? If I become his distro—"

"I have no problem placing my orders through Lorenzo. That is how it is supposed to be. It's time to fix the chessboard. The capacity of orders he would place with you not for only me, but the other boroughs as well, not to mention the other entities he does business with, will be at a high volume. This has the power to take you above and beyond. You could even get yourself a new office." Boogie looked around to add effect. "Do you think you could handle that?"

"Of course I can. But my question is, why are you offerin' this kind of deal to me and not Gino?" Tweety asked, looking from Boogie to Bentley.

"Gino's dead. But if he weren't, he would be the one in your position. Trust me on that," Boogie told him.

The two men gave each other hard stares. Boogie had come there to make a business deal, but he was also prepared to take what he wanted by force. Cousin or not, if Tweety wasn't willing to help Lorenzo, Boogie would appoint someone who would.

"Let's make it happen," Tweety said finally. "I'ma have your man meet my guy Sammie at the warehouse. We just got a new shipment in. If he likes what he sees, we're in business. How does that sound?"

"Sounds like we just made some shit shake."

Chapter 29

"All right. I just wrote it down. I'll see him tomorrow night then. Boogie, I don't know how I'll be able to repay you," Zo said into his phone.

"You should know that you don't need to pay me a thing back. Just tryin'a glue all this shit back together. Let me know how everything goes tomorrow."

"I will."

Zo disconnected the phone and punched the air in Marco's study happily. Boogie had come through exactly how he said he would. It was like a planet had gotten lifted from Zo's shoulders. He was a day late on giving Louisa an answer to her proposal. It was going to be a no regardless, but now he could put a little more umph behind it. After what his mother had told him about her, he didn't want anything to do with Louisa Alverez. Every word that had come out of her mouth was a lie. He pulled out his phone to call her, but right when he was hitting the call button, Daniella walked into the room. She had some papers in her hands and set them on the desk in front of him.

"We're completely out of oranges and strawberries. And it doesn't look like more are coming anytime soon. Lorenzo, I told . . . Why are you smiling like that?"

Zo was in such a good mood that there was a smile stuck in place on his face. Her words about them being out of supplies fell on deaf ears because it wouldn't be a problem for long. He took the papers and threw them away.

"What did you do that for? You didn't even look at them!"

"I don't have to. All of that shit will be fixed by tomorrow night."

"You finally agreed to Louisa's offer?" Daniella asked happily.

"No, I told you I wasn't going to do that. Something better happened. I found a new connect."

"You mean Boogie did."

"Same difference."

"Is it the same person who provided him with weapons when he was at odds with Papa?"

"Why does that matter, Daniella?"

"Because it does! How do you know they'll be able to provide us with what we need at the same capacity as Louisa?"

"I trust Boogie."

"Yeah, the same way Papa trusted Caesar, and look where that got him. Killed!"

"That's not what got him killed."

"Oh, yeah. I forgot. Boogie pissing off the Chinese is what got him killed! When are you going to choose your family?"

"Louisa is not our family!" Zo shouted so loud that Daniella stepped back from him.

"She is our aunt by blood. I've been talking to her and—"

"You've been talking to her?"

"Yes. She's here waiting on your answer, and I—"

"Why didn't you tell me?"

"I shouldn't have to tell you what you should already know. When she leaves, I'm going back with her. Papa left everything here to you anyways."

She'd complained about the same thing before, but that time Zo saw something that he didn't pay attention to the last time. There it was written all over her face and in her eyes, dripping from her tone. Envy. Zo stood up and tried to grab her hands, but she pulled away.

"When are you going to see that she is using your weakness against you, Daniella? She's turning you against me."

"No." Daniella shook her head. "You did that all on your own."

She stormed out of the study before he could stop her. He couldn't believe he had been so blind. She'd been giving him signs of her deep-rooted issues the entire time, but he was so wrapped up in himself that he didn't even see it.

"Dammit." He hit the desk with his fist.

The last thing he wanted to do was see Daniella anywhere near Louisa. He didn't know what kind of game that woman was playing, but she had his sister wrapped up in it. He was starting to think that her obsession with his father had passed to his kids. And if she couldn't have Zo, she would get Daniella. As much as he wanted to find Daniella and clear everything up, he had to cure the cancer. He dialed Louisa's number, and she answered on the first ring.

"You're here?" was the first thing out of Zo's mouth.

"You must have talked to your sister."

"I did. And she seems to think she's coming back to Florida with you when you leave."

"Really? I would love that."

"Well, keep dreaming. Because she won't be going anywhere. Especially with you."

"Where is this hostility coming from, Lorenzo? If you need more time to make your decision, just ask and I can give you some more time."

"Fuck you. Do you hear me? Fuck you. You crazy-ass bitch. You want to know my decision? It's no. I don't want anything to do with you. Or the money and businesses you gave my papa. My mama told me all about you."

"Your mother is delusional."

"No, you're delusional! And psychotic! When did they let you out, eh? I know all about what you tried to do to yourself and my papa when you were younger. What? Nothing to say now?"

There was a long stint of silence, and Louisa stared with an emptiness in her eyes.

"You know, you're not at all like my brother. I thought maybe, but no. You're not," Louisa finally said.

"Now I know for sure you and Daniella have been talking. That's all she reminds me of, but guess what? I'm just fine being Lorenzo Alverez. My papa raised me to be my own man."

"He raised a fool! The same fool aligning himself with the same motherfucker who got his father killed. Daniella told me all about Boogie and the feud with the Chinese. You have no loyalty to family."

"The thing is I do. And that's why this conversation is over. It will be a good idea for you to leave New York tonight."

He disconnected the phone and left his father's study, hoping that was the last he ever heard of her.

The phone was still to her ear even though Lorenzo had already hung up. Her bottom lip trembled, and madness fell upon her. He had just awakened a kind of rage that had been dormant inside of her for a very long time. She heard her father's and Gabriela's voices in her head as she thought back to one of the worst days of her life.

"We have to send her away, honey. She almost killed our son!"

"I'm sure she didn't mean to. She almost died herself."

16-year-old Louisa lay in a hospital bed, pretending to be asleep as she listened to her father and his wife bicker back and forth. It wasn't the first time they'd had a disagreement about her, but it was by far the most intense. She lay still so she could hear what the evil bitch had to say about her.

"You can't be serious. I know you see it too. How clingy she is to DeMarco! She poisoned their food!"

"He's the only one in the house who acts like he gives a damn about her! I'm out working all day. The least you can do is just talk to the girl."

"Don't you think I've tried bonding with her? She hates me! She put bleach in my soap, for crying out loud."

"She just wants some attention."

"No! This is it. She actually likes DeMarco and she did this to him. What do you think she'll do to my other children if we bring her back home, eh? No. She has to go someplace that can help her. Her mind . . . her mind is bad. She's not normal."

Louisa felt her fist balling up underneath the covers, but she didn't make a sound. She knew that her father wasn't going to send her anywhere. She was his responsibility since her mother died. Gabriela might not have liked her, but the one thing she couldn't change was that he was her blood. She was his family.

When Louisa came back to the present, she was blinking away tears because she'd been wrong. Her father did send her away to the worst place imaginable. Not even anywhere close that he could visit her often. The Marlene Institution in Florida. It was a place for troubled youth. She was forced to take medicine on a daily basis to the point where she didn't feel like herself. Some days she didn't know if she was alive or dead. Some days she hoped she *was* dead. Anything to not feel like unwanted trash. Like a waste of space. Not wanting to breathe . . . it was an experience she wouldn't wish on anybody. Her freedom was stolen from her for years until she was able to convince them that she was stable. She sold them the truth, or at least what they wanted to hear and see. But then again, she never thought there was anything wrong with her in the first place.

"I'm sorry things will have to end this way, dear nephew."

She was about to put her phone away when she saw another call coming in. That one was from Daniella. She cleared her throat and answered it as sweetly as she could.

"Hello, Daniella?"

"My brother has gone completely loco. Did he tell you?"

"Tell me what?" Louisa acted oblivious.

"I just wanted to give you a heads-up that Lorenzo has made his decision."

"Has he come to his senses?"

"No. He found someone new to provide what we need. He's meeting them tomorrow night."

That was news to Louisa. She thought that Lorenzo had blown up on her because of what Christina told him. But there was more. Boogie actually came through for him. Her jaw clenched tighter. No wonder he was so comfortable speaking to her in such a manner. He didn't need her anymore. Whenever someone didn't need her, they just threw her aside. Just like her ex-boyfriend. That was why she had to kill him and take over his business. He thought he was going to bring a new woman home, and now both of their bodies were swimming with the fishes.

"Louisa?" Daniella's voice brought her back to reality. "Are you still there?"

"Yes, I'm still here. How do you know he's meeting this new supplier tomorrow?"

"I saw a note on his desk and just put two and two together. I'll text you the time and address. Maybe you can intercept him and make one last offer?"

"Maybe. Because family is best together, right?"

"Right. If it's . . . if it's okay with you, I want to come back to Florida with you. Lorenzo already said he doesn't want Papa's businesses. Maybe I could run them? You know, make something for myself."

"That's fine with me. There won't be anything left for you here anyways."

Chapter 30

"Y'all can go on ahead and go home for the night! I'll handle it from here!" Sammie Donald's voice echoed in the large warehouse.

The workers around him had done everything they needed to do with Tweety's most recent shipment, and the only things that needed to happen now were orders and deliveries. However, it was getting late, and he had business to attend to that night. He stood next to an empty table looking down at a clipboard. He was marking a few items off when a man named Kai approached him.

"Where do you want these, boss?" In Kai's hands was a big and heavy-looking square box containing weapons.

"Lay them out right here. That's the stuff Tweety wanted me to show the motherfucka coming tonight."

"'A'ight," Kai said and placed the box down. He threw up two fingers. "I'll see you next week."

"No doubt. You and wifey have a good vacation! Stay safe."

"You do the same."

When Kai was gone, Sammie rubbed his thick beard and checked his watch. Tweety had trusted him with an important task. And if all went well, it meant big meals for everyone. Sammie loved money, especially the potential to make more. Lorenzo Alverez was coming to check out some inventory, and if all went well, and there was no reason why it wouldn't, then they would be providing weapons to not just one borough. They would be supplying them all.

"And my mama said I wouldn't amount to nothing," Sammie laughed under his breath.

He wasn't expecting Lorenzo for another half hour, the perfect amount of time to roll one and smoke it. He conducted business better when he was high, or at least that was what he told himself. After setting up the target that he was going to let Lorenzo test the guns on, he went out the back of the warehouse. It was where he and a couple of the other guys sat when they took their breaks. He reached in his pocket to grab the sack of weed and lighter he had with him. Instead, he pulled out an already-rolled blunt.

"I forgot I had this bitch. Today must be my lucky day," he said and lit it.

The smoke from the first drag filled his lungs, and he held it in before blowing it out. He closed his eyes for a few moments just to relish the feeling of going up. When he finally opened his eyes, the only thing he saw was a man with two braids standing in front of him and pointing a gun at his face.

"Ay yo, man. What the fuck? You aren't supposed to be in here!"

"I know. That's why I have the gun," the man said.

"Tweety is gonna kill you after he finds out you robbed him."

"Who said anything about robbing him?"

"Then what . . . what do you want?" Sammie asked, staring down the barrel of the gun.

The man didn't say anything. He just smiled slowly.

Adam had never killed anyone before on purpose. But with how much money Louisa was offering and the anger coursing through his veins, he would have murdered anybody. He hadn't even cared to get the man's name because he was nothing to Adam. Just a body. One that he had to hurry and dispose of before Lorenzo got there. He was able to dump the man in an empty crate in the back of the warehouse. He stacked a few more crates on top of it, and by the time he was finished, he saw headlights pulling up outside of the warehouse. He hurried to the front, where he'd seen the table of weapons, and stood next to it. He wiped his hands off and checked his new suit, happy to see that no blood had gotten on it. Minutes later, Lorenzo came walking in with a small army of men.

"Sammie?" Lorenzo asked Adam.

"In the flesh," Adam lied and smiled big. "Tweety told me you were coming through, and you're right on time."

He still didn't know what Louisa's endgame was, but she had provided him with a way of living he had only dreamed of in jail. His shoes alone cost the amount of what sent him to prison. Louisa had told him when and where to be that night. The objective was to knock Boogie's person off the board and pose as him. The next step was to make sure he placed an order. What Adam didn't understand was that if Lorenzo would really be placing an order through Louisa, wouldn't that put him back where he started from? He didn't understand it at all, but there had to have been a method to her madness. Especially if a part of it had to do with taking Boogie down.

"Being punctual is important to me," Lorenzo said. "If we are going to do business, I need to know that you will be on time with my orders."

"Of course. I can assure you of that."

"Just here in New York there is a high demand for what I provide."

"I understand that."

"I also provide weapons to many other entities. Do you think you'll be able to accommodate the volume of orders I will have?"

"I don't think there is any reason why we wouldn't be able to."

"Boogie seems to have a lot of faith in you, and I trust him. So I'm excited to see the kind of business we are able to conduct together. Are these your showpieces?" Lorenzo asked and made a move toward the table.

"Yes, take a look. That's not anywhere near all of what we have. As you can see, we just got a shipment in."

"I see," Lorenzo said, glancing around the full warehouse. "That's why it's strange that you're here alone."

"You think I'm here alone because you don't see anyone?" Adam asked.

He was remembering his last run-in with Boogie. He had underestimated him when really, he had shooters all around him. Lorenzo's lips turned up, and he nodded his head in a "touché" manner. Adam let out a small sigh of relief. Maybe he should have gone to school to be an actor, because he was killing it.

Lorenzo turned his attention back to the table of weapons and picked up the first one. Adam stared at it and hoped like hell that Lorenzo didn't ask him any specific questions about it or about any of them, to be honest. He only knew the basics: aim and shoot. Anything else would be over his head.

"This is a nice AR," Lorenzo commented. "Lightweight, fully loaded. Can I shoot it?"

"Be my guest," Adam said and pointed at the thick wooden target a short distance away from them.

Lorenzo positioned himself in front of it and squeezed the trigger of the gun. The recoil of the weapon made his shoulder jerk, but not much. His bullets hit each X on the target, showing Adam that he was an expert marksman. It went on like that until Lorenzo had shot every gun on the table, examined every explosive and tested every blade. When he was finally finished, he held out a hand to Sammie.

"I think you just got yourselves a new client," he said, smiling.

"I take it you liked everything."

"I did. Especially that Glock 43X. Lightweight, no recoil. I want to place a bulk order right away. Of everything on that table."

"My boss will be very glad to hear the sh . . . that he was able to make you happy."

Lorenzo was too busy digging in the inside pocket of his suit for a pen to hear Adam's slipup. After he wrote down his order, Adam stepped out of earshot to make a phone call.

"If you're calling me, I hope you have good news," Louisa said when she answered.

"I do. Good for you and good for me. I'm going to need the other half of my payment because I just closed the deal with Lorenzo."

"You have his order?"

"Yes."

"Perfect. Send it to me so I can get it ready. Let him know it will be ready in a week."

"A week? I'm standing in a warehouse full of boxes. He's going to wonder why he can't get them now."

"Tell him you have other orders before his, but assure him that he will get what he buys."

"Okay. And my payment?"

"You will get that plus more if you continue to play my game."

"Does more include Boogie's head on a stick?"

"Why, of course it does."

Chapter 31

Morgan couldn't help the nervous feeling in her stomach as she walked with Bentley through Times Square. She felt like there were ballerinas inside of it having an entire recital. They walked side by side on a sidewalk, and she didn't know if she should grab his hand or how to even let him know it was okay if he did. Before, she would have a million and one things to talk about with him, but things changed after they had sex. Now she felt like a schoolgirl around him.

"You good?" he asked from beside her.

"I'm fine," she said.

"You sure? Because I thought a shopping trip for our first date would have been right up your alley. But you've barely said five sentences to me."

He was giving her a strange look, and she wanted to just slap herself. He probably thought she didn't like him, and it was the complete opposite. She opened her mouth to say something but then shut it when she forgot what it was. Bentley had been a complete gentleman. He was polite, he held every door for her, and he even was carrying her shopping bags, so she didn't get what was happening to her. But she felt it. He made her knees want to buckle when he smiled. She wanted to bury her head in his neck and inhale his cologne. And she wanted to be the only one in the world to ever have his gaze.

Bitch, you're falling in love, she thought, but she shook the thought away.

No way could she have been falling for him that fast. There was just no way. For Bentley? Yes, he exceeded all of her expectations in bed, and yes, she liked him. A lot. But love? He glanced over at her again, and her stomach did flips instantly.

Okay, maybe I am falling for him. But how? What am I supposed to do? I can't even find my voice with this nigga. He probably thinks I'm on drugs.

"Are you sure you're okay?" Bentley asked.

"I'm fine. Just nervous I guess," she said and shook her evasive thoughts away.

"You? Nervous? Get out of here. I'd believe vampires were really in New York before I believed that."

"Why don't you believe me?"

"You're just one of the most confident women I've ever met," he said and gave her a knowing look. "Especially in bed."

"That's different. I let my body do the talking, and it always seems to know what it wants. But my mind is another thing."

"Don't tell me I done spent bands on you and you're about to hit me with the okey doke."

"No! That's not what I mean."

"Good, because I was about to give all this shit away on the street," he told her with a wink, and she laughed.

"You'd better not! I like that stuff."

"Well, how about we stop and grab some food so you can go more into detail about what you meant then?" he asked and grabbed her hand.

There were the butterflies again. She loved how take-charge he was. There was something about a dominant but kind man that made her kitty purr. He led her across the street to a nice Italian restaurant. When they got inside, the first thing Morgan saw was the crowd of people waiting to be seated.

"It's okay, Bentley. We can find somewhere else."

"We're good. Trust me." He winked at her.

The moment the host spotted him, he smiled big and waved the two of them toward him.

"Bentley! My man. Good to see you."

"Good to see you too, Raul," Bentley said and shook his hand.

"And you have somebody new with you this time."

Upon hearing those words, Morgan leaned back and gave Bentley the stank eye. "Don't have me in the same spot that you take all your other little girls," she told him seriously, and he laughed.

"There she is. I knew she was in there somewhere," he told her and flicked her chin. "And the only person I come here with is my sister. This is her favorite spot. I thought you'd like it."

"Yes, Roz," Raul butted in. "I haven't seen her."

"She hasn't been feeling too good, but I'll let her know you asked about her."

"Please do. She always makes me laugh when she comes. So a table for two today? Right this way."

"Mm-hmm." Morgan pursed her lips at Bentley, letting him know that the host had just saved him from the tongue-lashing of his life.

"Girl, I wouldn't bring you anywhere that I took somebody else."

The restaurant was busy, but Raul managed to seat them at a table with a little privacy. Bentley placed the shopping bags underneath the circular table as Raul placed their menus in front of them. When he was gone, their waiter came and poured them some water.

"Can I start you off with anything to drink besides water?" he asked.

"A Long Island please," Morgan said.

"Nothing for me," Bentley said.

"I'll give you two time to order, and I'll be right back with that Long Island."

When he was gone, Morgan looked around the restaurant. It was a comfortable place to eat, and it had the perfect view of Times Square. When her eyes swiveled back around to Bentley, she saw that he was watching her.

"What?" she asked shyly.

"I've just been wondering why somebody like you hasn't been snatched up yet."

"I guess I've just been busy with other things." She shrugged. "Hell, with everything that's taken place in my life, I barely have time to think."

"I feel you. This shit is fast-paced. But we're still here running the game," he said, and Morgan laughed. "What?"

"You just sound just like Boogie."

"That's my guy. Great minds think alike."

"Uh-huh."

The waiter came back with her Long Island, and as she sipped, she looked at the menu. It didn't take long for her to decide that she was going to get the lasagna. The picture next to the description had her mouth drooling already.

"So . . ."

"So?" she asked, fighting the smile coming to her face.

"Are you gon' tell me what you meant out there on the sidewalk or do I have to ask?"

"You're still on that?" she said and smacked her lips. She really had hoped he would let it go. She didn't want to sound like a simp on her first date. Or push him away for that matter.

"I wanna know. You've been acting shy around me all day. I mean, I know I'm that nigga and all, but—"

"Boy, bye! Not feeling yourself," Morgan turned her nose up, and that made him crack up.

"Nah, I'm playing. But for real. I wanna know where your head is at."

"It's with you," she answered honestly. "It's not a secret that I've been feeling you. And obviously you know that now."

"But?"

"Why does there have to be a but?"

"I don't know. That's just where it sounded like you were going with all that."

"No. It's just . . ." She shook her head. "You make me feel things I've never felt before. That sounds corny as hell, but I'm for real. You give me butterflies."

She lowered her head slightly, and her eyes fell to the white tablecloth. She felt naked. She'd left herself wide open, and she didn't even know if he felt anything for her other than physical attraction. She wanted to kick herself until she felt his hand under her chin lifting her head back up.

"I like eye contact when people talk to me," he said, and his thumb gently brushed across her bottom lip before he let her chin go. "You don't ever have to hide your feelings from me. A'ight? That's what I need to lead me to you."

"Okay. It's just hard for me to be so open when I don't know how you feel."

"You don't know how I feel?" Bentley asked, genuinely seeming shocked. "You must think I'm like these other niggas. Wining and dining every woman I meet. Sticking my dick into anything with a fat ass and pussy."

"I didn't say all that, but since you brought it up, are you?"

"I'm a man. Of course I've had my fair share, but pussy doesn't move me. Money and opportunity do. To be honest, I don't even know the last time I went on a date."

"Liar."

"For real. I be chilling, and plus . . ."

"Plus what?"

"You really been the only thing on my mind since that Stefano shit. You were sexy as hell to me that day. I knew I wanted you back then."

"So why didn't you say anything?" Morgan asked but already knew the answer. "Boogie."

"That's my mans. I didn't want to push up on his brand-new sister. I felt like it wasn't my place."

"But he's with Roz, and she's your sister."

"I've been a brother for forever. I know the motions that come with niggas getting at my sister. Boog's new to all of this. I didn't want to be disrespectful."

"But here you are."

"Yeah, 'cause you put that good-ass pussy on me."

His words made Morgan choke on her drink. She grabbed a napkin and dabbed her mouth dry. She sucked her teeth and tried to grow serious again.

"Is that the only reason you're here?"

"I just told you that I've been wanting you. That's just a bonus. I don't plan on letting you go anywhere soon if that's what you want to know. So cut all that shy shit and just be my baby."

It should have been illegal how much he was making her smile. By the end of the date she knew her jaws were going to be sore. In that moment, she was happy. And a piece of her wished she could stay there forever.

Chapter 32

Two Months Later

The sound of laughter and music filled the air. It was a beautiful sound to hear after what felt like a drought of happiness. The last time the Alverez backyard was filled with people was to say final goodbyes to Marco. Now it was filled for a celebration of continuous life. The weather had warmed up, and Zo wanted to take full advantage of it. He'd taken the liberty of putting tables and decorations out. Food was being cooked on the grill, and he was surrounded by people he cared about. All except Daniella. She had really chosen to go to Florida with Louisa, and it broke their mother's heart. However, Zo tried to respect her decision. She would see for herself soon what kind of person their aunt was, and until then he would love her from a distance.

Zo found himself in the kitchen with his mother, standing side by side cleaning corn cobs. She seemed happier that day than in the past days since Daniella left. He felt like it was because her house was full of people. Smiles had a way of brightening even the saddest of hearts.

"How have you been feeling, Mama?" Lorenzo nudged her playfully.

"I'm good as any old lady can get."

"You're not old," he told her.

"You'll say anything to make me happy." She winked at him. "Today is one of those days I wish your father were here to see. Oh, he would be so proud of you, Lorenzo. Look at what you've done. What all of you have done."

"Thanks, Mama. Have you talked to Daniella?"

"No," Christina sighed. "She hasn't answered my calls. I can't believe she ran off with that *bruja*. But I have to take some of the blame for it."

"You can't blame yourself for her decision. She's grown and made her choice."

"It is partially my fault if she felt that your father favored you. I told you before that he always put your name on everything because you were his heir, the one who would follow in his footsteps. But the truth is I might have forced him to do it that way."

"Mama, I don't get it."

Lorenzo stopped washing the corn. He didn't want to hear it the way it sounded because it seemed like she had picked favorites between her two kids.

"I know it sounds bad, but listen to me. I always knew who your father was and what might happen to him one day. And as you grew up, I knew right away you would follow in his footsteps. You were his better-looking half." She smiled and pinched his cheek lightly. "But Daniella? She was my princess. I never even wanted her to get her hands dirty if she didn't have to. DeMarco had his Mini-Me, and I just wanted one too."

"She was your Mini-Me."

"For a short time, yes." Christina shook her head. "But when she became a teenager, she wanted to be more and more like your father. She wanted to shoot guns and build them. And I always found her reading those weapons-parts books your father gave you to read. She would sneak them out of your room. I think it was the first time I caught her building a gun that made me do it."

"Made you do what?"

"I made DeMarco promise me that Daniella would have no part in his business dealings. He promised, but of course Daniella found a way around it. She was always so good with numbers. I should have just let her be who she wanted to be. But see, that's the flaw in mothers. We see *all* of the amazing things our kids can be, and when they choose our least favorite, we're disappointed. I think Daniella felt that in me sometimes."

"Don't say that, Mama."

"Why else would she leave home and go with somebody she barely knows?" Christina clutched her stomach and inhaled sharply to keep her tears at bay. "Louisa might not have gotten Marco back, but she stole a piece of him from me."

Zo pulled her close and rubbed her back in a comforting motion. She didn't sob, but he felt her tears drop on his arm. Nobody liked seeing their mother sad, but it broke him to see her cry. She'd lost so much, too much.

"Daniella isn't gone because of you. She left because of me and a decision that I made. She'll be back. Once she sees Louisa for who she truly is and the error of her own ways, she'll be back."

Christina pulled away and dabbed the remaining tears away with her hand. Zo watched her go back to washing the corn in silence. He wished he'd kept his mouth shut about his sister. For a moment there, it was like his mother forgot she was gone. Not knowing what else to say, Zo went back outside to the party. He grabbed a beer and walked to where he'd left Nicky to watch the meat.

"Ay, somebody get this motherfucka off the grill. He's burnin' the ribs!" Boogie's voice sounded, and he pointed at Nicky, who indeed was burning the ribs.

"I didn't ask to be on this shit anyway. Zo put the tongs in my hands and walked away!"

"If I had known you didn't know what you were doing, I wouldn't have," Zo laughed and approached them with a beer in his hand.

"Give those here," Boogie said and took the tongs from him. "This burnt-up-ass piece is yours."

"Bullshit. I came here to eat good, not like a peasant. Feed it to Bentley."

Bentley, who was sitting down at one of the tables with Morgan, looked up when he heard his name. He squinted his eyes at the three men suspiciously. It was obvious he didn't trust the smiles on their faces.

"What shit are you ugly-ass motherfuckas over there talking?"

"Boogie was just saying how his right-hand man deserves the first rib, that's all," Zo told him.

"Sike. I saw Nicky over there fucking up the meat. I was waiting for somebody to say something!"

Everyone laughed, and Nicky put up his middle finger. Bentley went back to saying what looked like sweet nothings in Morgan's ear, and Zo wondered if her cheeks hurt from smiling that hard. Boogie was staring at them too. Zo held back the smile that was trying so hard to come to his lips. It was obvious that Boogie was lost in thought and was on the verge of letting the ribs burn too. Lorenzo put his drink down and switched places with him so that he could tend to the food.

"You good with that, amigo?" Lorenzo asked, and when Boogie looked at him, he nodded his head toward the couple.

"I guess I don't have a choice, right? I mean, I'm with *his* sister, and he probably felt the same way that I'm feelin' at first. But . . ."

"But?"

"I just got Morgan. I guess I just wanted to have her to myself for a little while. And I keep thinkin' about what I would do if he hurts her. He's my boy and all, but she's—"

"Your sister. I know. I used to feel like that about Daniella. But you have to respect that she can make her own decisions. Once you do, shit will get a hell of a lot easier."

"You sound like a therapist," Boogie said and grabbed a beer from the cooler next to them.

"Maybe in another life, but I'm happy where I'm at."

"About that, I'm glad you got all squared away." Boogie tipped his drink to Zo.

"Me too."

"Me motherfucking three," Nicky chimed in. "I feel like shit is finally back to normal around here for once. Ming kept up his end of the bargain, and there hasn't been more violence than necessary out there."

"What kind of fucked-up world do we live in where a little violence is acceptable?" Zo found himself asking.

"A rich one," Nicky answered. "Either way, I'd say that's a win."

Zo had to agree. Business was booming, and he felt that his father would be proud of how he was handling things. For the first time since he had died, nothing seemed to be going wrong.

"Have you heard from Caesar?" Boogie asked Nicky.

"Here and there. Apparently, he and Diana are traveling the world together. Last I heard, they were in Mexico."

"Sounds like a blast," Roz entered the conversation, holding her daughter on her hip.

"Hey, baby," Boogie said and kissed her. He was about to give her another one, but his phone rang. "I'll be right back."

"What's up, Roz?" Nicky greeted her when Boogie left, and Zo nodded his head.

"Don't 'what's up' me. Y'all over here talking, knowing you're supposed to be cooking. Are the hot dogs at least done? Because homegirl is not nice when she's hungry."

Zo didn't believe her. Amber smiled big at him, and he didn't think she could be anything but a sweet angel. He pretended to squeeze her cheek, and she laughed.

"The hot dogs are right here. Help yourself," Zo said and held up a pan with cooked meat in it.

She started fixing Amber a hot dog, and by the time she was done, Boogie was walking back toward them. He had a strange look on his face. Zo figured it was because of whatever the phone call was about.

"You good, chief?" Nicky asked him.

"I don't know. I just got the weirdest call."

"From who?"

"Tweety."

"About what?" Zo asked, taking a swig of his beer. "I just placed another order through his man. Should be here any day now."

"That's the thing. Tweety said he's still waitin' to hear from you. What did you say his man's name was who you order through?"

"His name is Sammie. I don't know what Tweety is talking about. He's been supplying me for two months now."

"That's what you say," Boogie said, still looking flustered.

"Say? That's what I know. I invited him here today and . . . as a matter of fact, there he is."

Sammie stood at the patio door with Christina, who was pointing at them. Zo waved him over, and his mother went back in the house. Zo was too busy watching Sammie walk over to them that he didn't see the frozen look on Roz's face or the pissed-off look on Boogie's. Nicky, on the other hand, caught Boogie's vibe. Sammie stopped in front of the grill and casually nodded his head at them all.

"Everybody, this is—"

"I thought I told you to get out of New York," Boogie coldly cut Zo off. His words were directed at Sammie.

"I guess I'm just a little bad at following directions," Sammie replied.

"Yo, Zo. What the fuck is goin' on here? How do you know this nigga?" Boogie demanded.

"This is Sammie. I met him at Tweety's warehouse the night you told me to go."

"I don't know what warehouse you went to, but that ain't no Sammie."

"Hold on, hold on. If he's not Sammie, who the fuck have I been doing business with the past two months?"

"He's Adam. Amber's biological father," Roz spoke and tightened her grip on Amber.

The person Zo thought was Sammie shrugged his shoulders and chuckled.

"Well, I guess the jig is up. It was fun while it lasted. Sorry to disappoint you, Lorenzo. You're actually a pretty cool guy."

"Wha . . . why? How?" So many thoughts were going through Zo's head. He was beyond confused and didn't understand. "Who are you?"

"I'm Amber's father, like she said," Adam said and looked at the baby and smiled. "She has my nose."

Roz stepped closer to Boogie, who looked like he was about to explode at any second. And after one second, he did. His fist connected with Adam's jaw, dropping the man instantly. He repeatedly punched him in the face until Nicky pulled him off.

"Wait, Boog! Let's hear what he has to say. We've been getting our weapons faithfully, so he has to have somebody backing him."

It took both Nicky and Zo to get Boogie off of Adam. And when he did get off of him, the man had a busted lip and a bloody nose. Adam jumped up in an angry fit but didn't dare to make a move for Boogie.

"Why did you trick me?" Zo asked.

"Because I told him to," a voice that Zo knew all too well said loudly.

It was one that he had hoped to never hear again, but that was just too much like right. Louisa walked in the backyard with Daniella following closely behind her like a lost puppy dog. Accompanying them were two big men toting automatic handguns like it wasn't two in the afternoon. Louisa looked happy, like she was gloating. He didn't even know how she had gotten inside of the house to get to the backyard. Christina wouldn't have allowed it.

"Mama," Zo said and then glared at Louisa. "Where is she?"

"Get your panties out of a bunch." Daniella rolled her eyes. "She went to the store to get some tamales. She was so happy to see me she would have done anything."

"She saw you with her?"

"Of course not. I waited in the car until she left," Louisa told him.

"Zo, is that . . ." Boogie's voice trailed off as he looked at Louisa.

"Louisa, my aunt," Zo answered Boogie's question. "What do you want?"

"To see my plant, of course. And by plant, I mean him." Louisa pointed to Adam. "I sent him to the warehouse that night to pose as the person you were going to meet."

"Bullshit. There was no way you could have known I was meeting him unless . . . You! You told her." Zo stared at Daniella in disbelief. "Daniella, how could you? I'm your family."

"And she is too. Why couldn't you just see that, Lorenzo? She just wants what's best for you, and this? Them? They aren't."

"Things have been fine. Everything is back to normal!"

"Not for long," Louisa giggled and looked down at her red manicure.

"I got rid of you! I don't even fucking know you. You're just someone who shares the same last name."

"That hurts, Lorenzo, it really does. But do you think I was just going to let you get away that easy? You never got rid of me. Who do you think has *still* been supplying you these past few months?"

It clicked. The phone call Boogie received from Tweety. Adam pretending to be Sammie. It was all her doing. She had set him up. But it didn't make sense. He was still in Queens, not in Florida. So she still didn't get what she wanted. Louisa glared around at all of them, even Roz and Morgan.

"You, all of you are the reason my brother DeMarco is no longer here. He was the only thing that I ever loved, and because of you he is dead. You are foolish and incompetent to run any kind of business, and soon everybody will know that." She turned her attention back to Lorenzo. "You walk like him, you talk like him, but you do not love me like him. You broke my heart when you pushed me away. They always push me away."

"This bitch is crazy," Nicky said, giving Louisa a bewildered look.

"No, I am not!" she bellowed.

"Yes, you are, Louisa. You need help." Lorenzo shook his head at Daniella. "You brought her here, and she is unstable, Daniella. She needs help."

"No!" Louisa exclaimed and pointed her finger around. "You're going to need help. All of you will once it's found out that you sold defective weapons."

"What?" Lorenzo and Boogie asked in unison.

"Oh, yeah, did you think I had Adam supply you with weapons to prove my worth to you? You're so stupid. I did it to crumble everything around you and start another war. Now people will be coming at you from all sides." Louisa gave a psychotic laugh before abruptly becoming serious again. "I am just someone looking for something I lost and something I never had. But I'm learning that I will never get it, because he's gone. My brother is gone."

"You have me," Daniella told her. "I'm here. I won't leave you."

"Daniella . . ."

"Shut up, Lorenzo. She is the only person who ever saw me. I was invisible to all of you for so long. So long. I was invisible to everyone but her. I have power now. I'm a boss. With you, I was less than a street runner! You didn't even listen to me. Now you won't have anything."

"Papa built this. For us!"

"He built it for you! But it's like you have been saying— Papa is dead," Daniella said tearfully.

"Come to me, niece." Louisa held her arms out, and Daniella fell into them so she could comfort her. Louisa's gaze pierced Zo's with her next words. "You were some of the things that I thought Lorenzo would be. Except you're too much like your mother."

Lorenzo had been so focused on watching her lips move that he didn't see her remove a gun from the waistband of her pantsuit until the gunshot rang out. Daniella's head snapped to the side so hard that Zo heard her neck crack. She was dead before she hit the ground.

"Nooo!" Zo screamed and leaped toward Daniella's body. "Daniella! Daniella!"

Boogie and Nicky reached for their guns, but the men with Louisa already had theirs pointed at all of them. Louisa smirked and looked down at Lorenzo frigidly.

"Now we both know what it feels like to have our heart ripped out of our chest over and over."

Boom! Boom!

Zo jumped at the sound of the gunshots. He knew he would be joining his sister soon, but when he looked down at his body, there were no bullet holes. Suddenly he heard a bloodcurdling cry. It belonged to Roz.

"Boogie! No!"

Zo turned his head just in time to see Boogie falling to the ground and Adam standing over him, holding a smoking gun. Once he realized what he had done, he grabbed Amber and ran. Bentley tried to go after him, but the sound of automatic fire made everyone take cover. When it stopped and Zo looked up, they were gone. Bentley and Nicky ran after them. Morgan was trying to help Roz apply pressure to Boogie's wound while calling for help at the same time.

"Hello, there's been a shooting," Morgan barely was able to get out through her tears. "Please send help now. Wha . . . no! Send somebody now! My brother is dying!"

She hung up and went back to tending to Boogie. He was gasping for air, barely clinging to life. But he was fighting. Zo's eyes went to the blood on his hands and the blood in the grass. It was too much. He was tired of seeing it. What had started as the perfect day had ended in chaos. The final straw was seeing his mother step in the backyard, finally back from the store, and screaming because her daughter was lying dead next to a chunk of her brains.

Epilogue

The sound of the waves hitting the shore was therapeutic to Diana's nerves. She lay back in a chair, soaking up the sun and humming a tune she'd made up in her head. Of all the places she and Caesar had ventured to on their extended vacation, Tulum, Mexico, had by far been her favorite. She found herself lowering her sunglasses as a group of men half her age jogged by on the beach.

"Oh, to be young again," she said out loud.

"You're only as old as you feel," Caesar said, walking back to her in the sand. He'd gone to get them refills on their margaritas. He handed hers to her and took his seat next to her.

"Well, I feel old as hell," she said, taking a sip of the strawberry margarita.

"I don't. I feel like I could go jogging with those young fellas right now if I wanted to."

"Go do it then."

"I said if I wanted to." Caesar and Diana shared a laugh.

"Whew, this has been great." Diana smiled at the beautiful view before her. "We should have retired a long time ago."

"You think so?"

"No," Diana laughed. "New York would have gone to shit. But we're here now, and that means we did good."

"That we did."

When Diana first left, Morgan was calling her every day with something to do with the Sugar Trap or Harlem, but after a week, the calls stopped. It made her nervous at first, but then she realized that the training wheels had just finally come off. If she wanted Morgan to lead, then she would have to let her. But Lord knew it was hard for Diana to not check in. She fought the urge every day, and so far, she was doing good.

"I wonder how the kids are doing," she said absent-mindedly.

"The last time I talked to Nicky, everything was everything. They did it. They put the pieces back together."

"Except for the Bronx."

"They'll be back eventually. The boroughs are like Pangea. Time naturally will put them together again."

"Beautifully worded, my friend."

She closed her eyes and let her buzz take root. She and Caesar had agreed to visit two more places before going back home, and Diana had Greece set in her heart. She'd never been but had wanted to go since she was younger. She felt her eyes grow heavier and heavier until the sound of Caesar's phone ringing forced them open.

"It's Nicky," Caesar stated.

"Doesn't he know you're on vacation? If not, remind him!"

"Need I remind you that Morgan called you every day when we first left?" Caesar said with a grin, and she made a face. "Hello, nephew. I was just . . . What? Nicky, slow down. What happened?"

The change in his tone and facial expression made Diana set her drink in the sand and sit up straight. She strained her ears to hear what Nicky was saying, but the waves were too loud. Whatever it was, it wasn't good.

"Okay. We'll be on a plane out first thing. Try to hold it together."

When Caesar got off the phone, he stood up and tried to catch his breath. Anger took hold of him as he paced, and he launched his margarita into the sand. Diana knew something was drastically wrong when he covered his face and dropped back down into his seat helplessly.

"Caesar, what's wrong?" she asked and tried to brace herself.

"It's Boogie. He's dead."

Caesar's words echoed in her head over and over, and she tried to make them out differently every time. But the end result was all the same. There was no bracing for those words. There was only one thing she could do. Diana screamed.

Stay tuned for the final installment of *Carl Weber's Five Families of New York,* coming soon.

Other Books by C. N. Phillips

The Last Kings

The Last Kings 2

Deep

Hood Tales

Kingpins Los Angeles

Me And My Girl

Full Figured 12

Kingpins Harlem

The Nightmare on Trap Street

Five Families Book 1: Brooklyn

Five Families Book 2: Harlem

The Education of Nevada Duncan Book 1

Five Families Book 3: The Bronx